the
Other
Girls

the
Other
Girls

Lola Pridemore

Reverberator Books

For Little P

Paperback ISBN-13: 978-0-9837050-6-2
Paperback ISBN-10: 0-9837050-6-2

Published by Reverberator Books.

eBook ISBN–13: 978-0-9837050-3-1
eBook ISBN–10: 0-9837050-3-8

Bancroft House

The children were hungry. They always were. The pangs caused their stomachs to growl and throb. It had been this way for a while now, ever since their father had died.

The three girls sat across the rickety kitchen table from their mother, who refused to make eye contact. Her teeth were clenched as she stared at the wall with a mixture of disgruntlement and grief. The girls couldn't tell if she was angry at them or just angry in general. Nevertheless, they felt her emotions so strongly it was as if they, too, were experiencing them. Not for one second, however, did any of them question why they were in this predicament. None of them asked "Why me?" or even said, "I'm too young for this." They accepted their fate, and the fact that their mother was doing this to them, as they accepted the oxygen in the air. There was no recourse. It was the way it was and the way it was meant that their lives were going to change very, very soon. And probably not for the better.

"Mommy?" Adele, the eldest, said.

Her mother, without looking over at her, muttered, "Yeah, honey?"

"We can—"

"No, we can't!" her mother half-yelled. "Girl, I've told you, it has to be this way. I can't do it. I'm sorry, I just can't. Not without your daddy, I can't. I just can't."

Adele's eyes dropped to the surface of the table. Her eyes traced the grain in the old oak until they formed a pattern of a big circle, then she traced it back again and then again until her eyes blurred. She stopped for a moment and stared at her younger sisters, Eliza and Cecilia. The girls looked a lot like her. They were small girls, ages six and eleven, and though their cheeks were gaunt from days of not getting enough to eat, they were beautiful. Their long, black hair lay straight against their backs and their gray-blue eyes, framed by thick black eyelashes, tried to come to an understanding of what their mother was doing. Their pale faces were sprinkled with freckles here and there and gave observers the impression that these girls had spent some time in the sun, and they had. They had all grown up outside working in the garden and doing what needed to be done in order to have food for winter. However, this winter had been different. This winter had brought with it a new reality and that reality was the fact that without a man around helping them there would be very little food.

Adele resented this. She knew what was going on. She hated it, hated the fact that her father had been killed in the mines of West Virginia only a year prior. The irony was that he had just gotten the job as a miner a few months before and was finally making decent money and the girls were bound for a better life because of it. But that had quickly come to an end. Now, they were bound for something entirely different. Besides that, they loved their father and his sudden death had a huge, negative impact on all three of them. He had been a kind man, tall and handsome, funny and generous. Life with their father had been fun and he had a knack of bringing out the best in his girls. He loved his daughters and his wife. Loved them so much he would work overtime every week just to give them special little treats. Now there were no more special little treats. Life had turned cold, hard and bitter.

Adele knew this. She was fourteen, going on fifteen. She knew she was beautiful, as were her sisters. She was the perfect combination of her parents who were thought to be the best looking couple in the county. But she also knew that her beauty didn't make much of a difference, at least not at her age. She didn't know anything about marrying up or that she could eventually use her beauty for betterment. All she knew was that she was poor and once you're pegged as poor, that's how people would always regard you. No, you couldn't outrun poor; it left a stench on you, like a black mark that lingered even if you got rich. Once someone called you poor, then that's what you were. You couldn't argue with fact even if many people in the county would say, "Those Clemmons girls are the prettiest things I've ever laid eyes on!" Beauty, when sullied with poverty, just didn't make much of a difference. At least not now.

This frustrated Adele. It ate at her and made her think bitter, mean thoughts. But she so young. There just wasn't much she could do about anything. But how she wanted to do something! How she wanted to turn that frustration into resolution and save her little family. Times had been tough since her father had died, but she knew, in her heart she *knew*, that things could get better. If only she would be given a chance at something she could make it right. But the underlying fear she had of what was to come made her want to run. She felt it so strongly it nearly nauseated her.

"Mommy," she started again. "Let me do something. It doesn't have to be this way."

Her mother, weary from the anguish, overwrought from grief and so worn out from trying to raise three young girls on her own, allowed her shoulders to slump. She was *this close* to bursting into tears. She had gotten a job but, because of her qualifications, which were pretty much nonexistent, the pay was low and just didn't cover the bills, let alone food and clothing for the girls. It had been a long year since her husband's death and she had done what she could. However, it was all over, and that included the crying. She had no tears left. She knew that, probably, she'd regret her decision, but it was better than allowing her children to starve and to go without. Anything was better than that and for that reason, she stood by her decision.

"Mommy," Adele said. "I know I can do something."

Her mother finally lifted her head and met her eyes. She couldn't help but smile at her oldest daughter, at her beauty, at her young face. She remembered the day she was born. After a hard labor, her husband had taken her hand and stared down at the baby in her arms. He smiled at her lily white skin and the thick black hair on her head. "She looks like a little Indian, doesn't she?" he said proudly. "She looks like my grandmother Hopper. Don't she?" She had agreed and was pleased that he had noticed. The Cherokee blood had been strong in Adele and her sisters. She only hoped that the blood would give them the strength that they needed in order to survive. But she didn't want to think about that right now. Right now, it was time. It was time to take action and time to get moving.

"Mommy?" Adele said, almost giving up on ever being answered.

"Shh, baby," she replied, feeling the tears sting the back of her eyes. "You know we have to go now. I'm sorry. But we have to."

Adele watched in horror as her mother rose from the table. It was going to happen now, there was no doubt. It was really going to happen. Her mother was going to go through with it. And there wasn't a thing Adele could do to save herself or her sisters. For a split second, she regretted her decision not to run away. She regretted her decision to stay and see if she could change her mother's mind. She regretted it because now she knew she had made the wrong choice.

She tried one last time, "Please Mommy, we can make it work."

Her mother shook her head once, finalizing the deal. Adele knew she was committed to doing it and once you get committed to doing something, there's nothing to stop it from happening. The door was not just closing; in fact, it had been shut for a while now.

The house the girls grew up in was very small, only two bedrooms. Their parents occupied the smaller of the two and all three girls bunked up in the other which was, by most people's standards, about the size of a McMansion's walk-in closet. However, their mother had painted the walls pink and tried to give the room a little updating here and there with curtains bought at thrift stores, vintage children's art and chenille bedspreads for the full size bed they all slept in together. While the room was small, it was pleasant.

The house itself was an older A-frame that their father had rented just before Adele had been born. The house sat on about two acres of ground and in the summer there was plenty of room for the girls to run around and play. A large vegetable garden sat a few hundred yards from the back porch and to the left of that, near the front, their mother had a flower garden and grew everything from roses to sunflowers. She would tell her children, "Just throw the seed in the ground, girls, and let God do with it what He will."

They loved to plant the seeds and watch with rapt attention as they sprouted and then grew into a tiny plants and then into flowers. The summers were always filled with lots of activity. The planning and then planting of the vegetable garden was the most important. It was a little less haphazard than the planting of the flowers. The girls were required to help plant, weed and tend to the garden. Adele loved this the most. She loved to go into the cucumber patch, pluck a fresh cucumber off the vine and then peel it. The sweet taste of sun that soaked into the cucumber gave her taste buds just a smidge of what heaven might taste like. When she would look back at this time in her life, she would always remember the cucumbers the most. There was nothing like a sun-warmed fresh cucumber to her. Her two sisters would remember the small house, the love from their parents and the warmth of the coal burning stove in the living room during the winter. They would remember the anticipation of Christmas morning and the smell of fried green tomatoes in the summer. The memories of this time in their life would haunt all three girls for some time. They would think of what used to be and wonder what might have been different in their lives had things turned out a bit differently.

Now, as they stood in front of the rock behemoth known as Bancroft House, they had no idea what lay in store for them. And they didn't much want to find out. However, they didn't have much choice. They turned to their mother with worried expressions, then glanced at the old brown station wagon that they'd never see again. Their mother had worried the whole trip, all twelve hours of it, that the car might just up and die on the way there, to this boarding school, located somewhere in Tennessee. They felt as if they'd not only been driven to another state but to another world.

The girls looked back to the school. Bancroft House was the biggest building, much less house, they'd ever seen. It was *huge*. The girls didn't know about the Edwardian style or the fact that it had only been turned into a school many years ago after the man who started to build it, Albert Bancroft, lost part of his prominent insurance business and had to shut down construction. He had owned agencies throughout Eastern Tennessee and even into Georgia. But once his business started to slide due to bad decisions, the construction of the house came to a standstill. That explained why there was an elaborate pool house, which actually housed offices now, and no pool. That would explain the ornate moldings throughout the monstrosity. To say that this house was large was like saying the clouds in the sky were high. It was gigantic in every sense of the word. And the former owner, once rich beyond imagination, had spared no expense. The kitchen was huge, as big as a normal person's whole house and the floors were beautiful herringbone oak. The baths, most of which had been converted into dormitory-style bathrooms with five sinks, five toilets and five showers, were outfitted in pristine white marble. The massive downstairs rooms had floor to ceiling windows and gigantic marble fireplaces with ornate statues of Greek goddesses holding up the mantles. Some were big enough to walk into.

To say that Albert Bancroft had gone all out was an understatement. However, when the man ran of money to finish the house, like any good businessman, he found a solution—donate it and turn it into a school for girls. Not an orphanage, per se, but a school where girls could come and stay and learn and flourish. This gave him a huge tax break and he went on to thrive in other businesses but still made a good impression by donating something that had taken almost eight years to build and another two to convert, with funds generously donated by interested parties, of course, into a proper boarding school.

The Clemmons girls did not know what to think or how to react to the school. It was too big, too imposing and too intimidating. It stood alone in front of wooded area and the surrounding trees were alive with bright fall colors. The two oversized stone lions on either side of the entrance were a little scary, too, and though they didn't know what the things perched on the roof were called, the gargoyles were not only frightening but terrifying. Their hearts were beating rapidly inside their chests and their mother, dressed in her Sunday best, seemed to hesitate before she pushed them forward, up the walk and into the big double oak doors of the school. Maybe she did pause and reconsider. Maybe she had thought about solutions to the problem as she drove all the way there. But then again, maybe not.

"Let's go," she said faintly and gave Adele a little push which got her and her two sisters going.

Soon, they were at the front door and before she could ring the bell, an older woman with a tight bun and brown tweed skirt and jacket, brown shoes, and brown hair opened the door.

"Mrs. Clemmons!" she said as if she knew their mother well. "I'm Head Mistress Tanner."

Their mother held out her hand and the two women briefly shook hands. "Nice to meet you," she told the woman. "These are my girls. The oldest is Adele, the middle one is Eliza and the little one is Cecilia."

The head mistress stared at the girls for a long moment before giving them a tight smile. It was almost as if she were setting the precedent for their future relationship. It was okay if they knew who she was; but it was not okay for them to be friendly with her or to expect anything from her, especially sympathy. It was almost as if this were some sort of business transaction and not an introduction to the school via the head mistresses.

"Please come in," she said and turned back to their mother. "We've been waiting on you!"

The girls took a moment to glance at one another before they entered the house. Once inside, they took another moment to gasp at the richness of the interior. The only words in their vocabulary to describe such opulence was "fancy," and "really, really nice." But, somehow, they knew that didn't even cover it. The girls had never been exposed to such wealth and really didn't even know it existed. The hallway seemed a mile long and the gigantic mahogany hall table that greeted them held the most beautiful bouquet of flowers they'd ever laid eyes on. They could identify some of the flowers—lilies, cannas, and even a mum thrown in for the fall—but some were unrecognizable to their eyes. And they knew about flowers.

The head mistress led them down the hall a bit and then to the left. She paused at a classroom and pointed into it. "This is our fourth-year class. They're studying history right now, pre-revolution."

Adele peered in and surprised herself at how interested she was. She'd always loved school, always wanted to go and learn everything she could. In a way, she couldn't wait to be done with all this and get back to school. She knew it would take her mind off her worries as well as give her something constructive to do. She stared at the girls in the classroom, all of who looked very clean, very neat, and even very rich to her. They were listening to the teacher with rapt attention and didn't even notice Adele or her sisters staring at them through the double French doors.

"Come along," the head mistress said and started off down the hall again.

Her mother nodded at them and they followed her into an office and stood by the door until the head mistress gestured for them to sit down on a brown leather sofa while their mother took one of the two chairs in front of her wide, heavy wood desk.

"Okay, let's see," she said, sitting down. "Mrs. Clemmons, would you say that the girls are up to date in their studies?"

"Of course they are," she said, a little taken aback. "Adele has always been at the top of her class and Eliza is really good in math and, of course, Cecilia, just got out of kindergarten but she's very smart, too."

Head Mistress Tanner nodded briefly, then said, "Let's just get on the paperwork, shall we?"

The girls sat there the better part of the afternoon while her mother and the head mistress completed all sorts of paperwork for their admittance. Adele looked around the wood-paneled office and at all the art work—horses and small rivers, mostly—and at all the furniture—bookcases filled with boring looking books, a few wood filing cabinets that looked really old and a few knickknacks like little porcelain birds. The office bored her. She couldn't stop thinking about the class. She was dying to get in there and learn something. She loved learning, loved reading. She read everything she could get her hands on, even these old detective novels her mother read constantly.

Maybe it might not be so bad, she thought to herself and almost smiled. And it might not be. The girls she had seen in the classroom looked really nice and she was sure they had a vast library filled with all kinds of interesting books. And the house was beyond anything she'd ever expected. And the way the head mistress explained everything to her mother, it sounded like one of the best schools in the state, possibly even in the country.

Just as they were finishing up the paperwork, her mother asked, "And, so, what exactly will the girls do here?"

"Well," the head mistress said. "As we've discussed previously, they're here on scholarship, so they will be treated like all the other girls. This means, they will be expected to clean up after themselves and help in the kitchen and whatnot."

"Like a work scholarship?" her mother asked.

"Yes, exactly," she said. "And with that, all the girls will have all rights and privileges as the other girls."

Her mother smiled with relief. "Good. That sounds great. I was so worried that they might be treated differently because of the scholarship thing. But knowing that they'll be treated the same as everyone else makes me feel better."

"Oh, they will be," the head mistress told her with what seemed like a sly smile. "They will be treated just like all the other girls."

"Well, I guess that's it," she said and turned to stare at her children. "Girls, I'll get going now."

They stood and went to her. She bent at the waist and held each of them in a long hug before kissing their cheeks and foreheads.

"I love you, girls," she said softly. "Be good and always listen to what Head Mistress Tanner has to tell you."

"We will," Adele promised. "We'll all be good, Mommy."

"I know you will," she said and smiled at her. "Want to walk me to the car?"

The head mistress stood up quickly and said, "It's not advisable to take them out with you, Mrs. Clemmons. We wouldn't want them to start crying and make a scene in front of the school. You go on now and I'll take them to the dining room. It's time for supper."

The girls' interest was piqued. After months of hunger, the thought of a meal was more than enough to take their mind off their mother's imminent departure. Adele even thought to herself, "Maybe this won't be so bad," then immediately chastised herself for forgetting about her mother. Part of her wanted to be excited, even happy, at the prospect of being at such a fine boarding school, but another part of her wanted her to feel guilty over her mother. Where would her mother go? Back to the old house? What would she do? Keep her job or get another one? What kind would she get? A job as a waitress? As a maid? As a clerk in the grocery store? Would it cover the bills for herself and, if not, what would she do about that? Would she ever meet a man and decide to marry again and, if so, would the union bring any new children? And, more importantly, when would she come back and take them home? There were too many questions left unanswered and her young mind grappled with the confusion of not understanding any of it.

"Oh, okay," her mother said. "Well, I'll be going, then."

Adele almost cried but then managed to hold it back. She wanted to be strong for her mother. Then she found herself being pulled closer to her mother who whispered very quietly so no one else could hear, "I'll be back to get you girls soon. I promise. Keep your sisters safe."

Adele nodded at her that she understood; her mother nodded back and pulled away and, without another word, she slipped through their arms and out the door, closing it softly on her way out. Adele stared at the door and got an ominous feeling that she'd never see her mother again. She shook it off and turned to the head mistress who stood staring at the door before turning to her. Once she did Adele felt shivers go up and down her spine. The woman's whole demeanor changed. While her mother had been there, she'd been nice, pleasant even. Now she seemed cruel, hateful. It was as if she'd seen her real face. Her father had once said something to her that had always stuck in her mind. After a big argument with one of his friends, he had told her, "There are two kinds of people in the world, Adele. The kind that are born mean and the kind that are made mean."

Adele realized that this woman was born mean. But that might not be true. Adele shook herself. Her mother had always told her to think the best of people and perhaps she was wrong about the woman. She decided she was, mainly because it wasn't to her benefit to think otherwise.

But the suspicious feeling she got from Head Mistress Tanner told her that she should have run after her mother and convinced her not to leave her and her sisters at this place. But it was too late. Her mother was gone and there was no way to get in contact with her, at least not until tomorrow when she got home from the trip. And even then, Adele didn't know if they'd even allow her to call her. For a moment, she felt a strong sense of urgency, of panic. But she couldn't let it cloud her judgment. *Things will be fine*, she told herself. *I have to be strong for my sisters.*

"Let's go," Head Mistress Tanner said and walked around the desk, to the door and opened it.

The girls followed her to the dining room without a word. They were ready to eat and ready to see what lay in store for them. They walked down the hall and within a minute, heard the sounds of clattering dishes and the voices of the girls having late afternoon conversations. They stopped at a double door and the head mistress pushed it in the middle and into the wall. Pocket doors. Adele was mystified as she had never seen anything like this. She was further mystified when she saw all the girls eating. There were two long tables that were jam-packed full of girls varying in age from about six to seventeen. The girls wore uniforms of plaid skirts, white button down shirts, which were fastened at the neck with a little black tie, knee socks and black leather mary-janes. They looked perfect, as if something from a movie or a storybook. Their hair was perfectly coiffed in ponytails, pigtails or braids, all adored with bright ribbons or pretty tortoiseshell barrettes. Their skin was clear and glowing.

Adele suddenly felt intimidated by these girls. But then, the aroma of the food was overpowering. The girls were eating what looked like pot roast with delicious looking homemade rolls and steaming green beans and mashed potatoes. They were drinking either water or big, tall glasses of cold milk. The girls picked at the food, ate a few bites here and there and then would put down their forks as if they couldn't be bothered. They certainly hadn't even acknowledged that the Clemmons girls had even entered the room with the headmistress.

Cecilia spied an empty seat and started to head to it when the head mistress grabbed her by the shoulder and held her back.

"Oh, no, no, no," she said. "You will be eating with the other girls."

The other girls? The three sisters turned to stare at another part of the large room which seemed to be invisibly roped off from the chattering, happy girls. The group of girls they stared at was not happy looking in the least and not really talking, either. They all looked sad and their clothing reflected this. The girls, about twenty or so of them, all sat straight with downcast eyes at a long table. They, oddly enough, weren't dressed as well as the girls at the other two tables. They were dressed in plain gray shirt dresses, short socks and beaten up looking mary-jane shoes that looked like castoffs. Their hair was all pulled back in tight ponytails but no ribbons. They looked, in a word, downtrodden.

"Now, go," the head mistress said and nodded her head at the table.

Adele turned briefly to her and felt a flash of anger. She, again, felt very leery about the head mistress and realized that she was the sort of person who not only instilled fear but turned fear into terror. Adele could tell that. She could also tell that she and the head mistress would more than likely bump heads in the future, too.

The head mistress nodded again at the table, telling them with her eyes to sit down and shut up. Adele knew it wouldn't be worth asking any questions, so, she put her arms around her sisters.

"Come on," Adele said and led them to three empty places at the far end of the table. When they sat down, none of the girls even looked at them. The head mistress gave each of them a short nod, turned on her heel and left the room. As soon as she left the girls seemed to relax and breathe a sigh of relief.

A girl around Adele's age stared at them and gave a weak smile. Adele stared back and wondered who she was, noticing her dark hair and lovely porcelain skin. She was a pretty girl who looked smart because she wore what Adele's father called "nerd glasses." They were black framed and were a little big for her face, but somehow, she made them work. They even looked hip, a term her mother used often. In fact, the glasses looked so stylish, they might have been worn by one of the girls at the other tables.

The girl shrugged, leaned across the table and said, "They're the rich girls. Don't even look at them. They're trouble."

Was she serious? Adele couldn't tell, but she had to look now. She glanced across her shoulder to stare at the girls again. They all looked prim and proper and, well, rich. She didn't know what distinguished them, other than their clothes, from the other girls. But there was something that made them different. Yes, they had an air about them, an aloofness that made her a little nervous and a lot intimidated. From their heads to their toes, everything about them screamed perfection and for that, Adele felt a little jealous. She observed them again and studied their demeanor and their looks. Their hair, whether it was curly or straight or wavy or blonde or brunette or red, was shiny and perfect. Some of them had pretty gold earrings or an interesting looking bracelet. If they wore glasses, they were stylish and expensive looking, as were their matching identical leather mary-jane shoes.

Adele took a moment to look down at her own shoes which were leather lace-up and very worn out. She'd gotten these shoes two years earlier after her mother had found them at a thrift store. Even then she'd thought they were the ugliest shoes around and was relieved when they had been too large for her to wear. Unfortunately, instead of throwing them out or even giving them to someone else, her mother had put them up in the closet and when her feet had grown to adequate proportions to fit the shoes, she'd pulled them out and said with a smile, "Thank God, I didn't get rid of these. They'll fit you perfectly now!"

Adele groaned inwardly. She'd never be able to outrun those shoes. They would mark her now. Even with the other girls, whose shabby shoes were even better than hers, though not much.

Just then, a plate of food was plopped down in front of them. Adele and her sisters pulled back to study it, then turned to watch the girl who'd delivered it scurry towards a swinging door and into what Adele suspected was the kitchen.

The girl leaned across the table again. "That's Lizzie. It's her night to serve."

Adele narrowed her eyes at her. What did she mean by that?

"We each take turns, three of us a night," the girl said. "We serve the food."

Adele nodded.

"Eat up," she said. "Oh, by the way, I'm Lotta."

Adele didn't bother introducing herself or her sisters. That's how hungry she was. However, the food was dull, to say the least and so different from the rich girls' food it made Adele want to cry. Plain beans and rice and a block of cold cornbread and plain water served in a tin cup. Adele stared at the food and, for a moment, felt a little like Oliver Twist. She shook the feeling off and wanted to dive in, even though the food was less than spectacular. She was about to do just that when she noticed her sisters had already started eating and were gobbling down the meal as if they hadn't eaten in days. And, really, they hadn't. Their mother had made only a few stops on the long trip to Bancroft House—bathroom breaks and gas stops. On one of the gas stops, she had given Adele a little money to buy some food but the all the old gas station offered was some stale donuts and prepackaged peanut butter and crackers. She had bought as much as she could with the five dollars and she and her sisters had eaten every last crumb. That had been over six hours ago.

Adele noticed that the other girls were watching them and she grew embarrassed for her sisters and elbowed each of them to slow down before they were belittled. They paused for a moment, realized what they were doing and ducked their heads in shame.

Just then, Adele noticed a tall redheaded girl sitting at the end of the table. The girl started smiling at them and shaking her head so fast that the thick mane of hair bounced on her head. Then she started smacking her lips and rubbing her stomach. The girl was obviously making fun of them and Adele got a protective urge to slap the girl just to wipe the smile off her face.

"Hungry?" she asked with a laugh.

Eliza and Cecilia grew embarrassed and stopped eating altogether. Adele glared at the girl.

"When was the last time you ate?" she asked, not in an unfriendly way.

"What's it to you?" Adele snapped. "Mind your own business."

"Oh, oh, that accent," the girl said and laughed even more. "*Where* are you from?"

Adele stared at her. She didn't know if she could trust her. She didn't know if she should, even enough to answer her question. This girl could be trouble. She thought it would be best to ignore her.

"Huh?" the girl asked again, not allowing herself to be ignored. "Where are you from? Not around here, that's for sure."

"Reckon?" Adele said sarcastically and tried to contain her eyes roll.

The girl stared at her for an instant, then squealed with laughter. "'Reckon?' What's that? I don't reckon I understand!"

As the girl collapsed into laughter, all the other girls smiled along with her, but didn't laugh themselves. It was as if they were afraid to bring attention on themselves. However, the redhead couldn't help herself. She almost bellowed with laughter, which seemed just a little spiteful. To say that Adele was taken aback would be a gross understatement. She stared at the girl, at her apparent condensation and wondered how she'd even gotten in this situation. Then she understood what the girl was doing. She was making fun of her Appalachian accent. And the girl had a thick southern accent herself, so who was she to try and embarrass her for the way she talked? Just because her accent was different didn't mean the girl was better than her. That was one thing her father had always taught her, that no one was better than her or her sisters, even if they thought they were. This didn't set well with Adele and she turned away from her.

"Oh, you must be from the mountains," she said, further taunting her. "You must be a mountain girl."

"Leave me alone," Adele said. "I mean it."

"I'm the welcoming committee," she said, trying to sound sarcastic. "That's all. I'm here to welcome you to Bancroft House. I'm Jane."

"Nice to meet you, Jane," Adele said. "Now leave me alone."

She started to say something else, then thought better of it and kept her mouth shut, which was probably for the best. Adele noticed that Eliza was staring at the girl, narrowing her eyes at her. Eliza wasn't the type to say much, but when she didn't like someone, she didn't hide it. Adele knew she was about to say something to the girl, but also knew she had to stop her.

"Eat," Adele told her, nodding once at her plate.

Eliza nodded and went back to eating, occasionally sneaking a look at the girl as if she were trying to figure out what needed to be done with her. Adele ignored her and glanced around the table a few times at all the other girls.

They all seemed to wear not only the same dull clothes, but the same dull expressions. It was as if the life had been sucked out of them so much that their skin was starting to resemble the dull gray of their uniforms. The girls could have been pretty had they been smiling or even glad to be in the world. But they were the unhappiest looking bunch of girls Adele had ever been around. These girls were pitiful. Adele felt a strong sadness for the girls. *What was going on? What was going on?*

They were almost finished eating when, all of a sudden, another woman entered the room. She was younger than Head Mistress Tanner and more slender. But she still had the same presence and stern look as the head mistress and she was dressed in pretty much the same outfit. Adele took a moment to note the true ugliness of the brown tweed.

"Ms. Ingles," Lotta told her. "She supervises us and tells us what to do. She kind of oversees us."

"Girls," Ms. Ingles said, addressing the rich girls. "It's time."

Adele watched as the rich girls stood and filed out without even tossing a look in the other girls' direction. It was as if they were truly invisible to them.

The other girls sat still, waiting. As soon as the rich girls were all gone, Ms. Ingles snapped her fingers and there was a sudden, loud creak of forty or so chairs against the floor as they were pushed back from the tables and the girls rose out of their seats. Then there was a flurry of activity. Adele and her sisters sat watching as the other girls hurriedly and methodically cleared the rich girls' plates, wiped their tables, pushed their chairs in place and swept the floor.

Jane paused and stared at them in frustration. "What are you doing?" she asked. "Get over here and help us!"

Adele and Eliza glanced at each other then raced to the tables where they helped clean. Adele noticed that the food, much of it, was barely touched and she longed to grab a fresh baked roll and shove it into her mouth. She didn't dare though, as she knew that would set the precedent of what the other girls would think of her. She didn't want to be known as the girl who was so hungry she'd eat food off of a stranger's plate. But she wanted to and she didn't hesitate to admit this to herself. But, as far as anyone else was concerned, she'd rather die than have them know she was that poor. There was so much shame in it for her that she didn't even take into account that the other girls were as poor, or perhaps even more poor, than she. Regardless, she didn't want them to know exactly where she stood. So, she ignored the food and prayed her sisters would do the same.

It took about ten minutes to clean the dining room and then the girls went into the kitchen where a few were already busy washing dishes. Adele didn't know what to do, so she and Cecilia and Eliza stood back and watched as the girls, with military precision, washed, rinsed, dried and put up the dishes. She noticed a lot of the other girls were doing the same thing as it only took about half of them to perform the duty. She wanted to ask questions, like why were they doing this stuff but she felt it was best to keep quiet. But what was going on? Why were they cleaning like this? But then she remembered Head Mistress Tanner telling her mother that they were here on work scholarship. This must be part of it.

Soon enough, they were done. Once they were, Ms. Ingles came into the room, inspected the dishes, nodded once and went to the door. The girls lined up single file and followed her. They were led down a long hall and into a big room filled with washers and dryers. There were about six washers and they were all going at full speed.

"Laundry," Lotta said whispered quietly into Adele's ear. "Every three days it's laundry day. We do it after supper."

"Oh," Adele said, wondering, exactly, why they were doing all this stuff. Sure, they might all be on work scholarship, but this was a little extreme. Wasn't this supposed to be a school? It was like she and her sisters were now some sort of child laborers. It didn't make sense, not after what she'd been told by her mother and by Head Mistress Tanner. Even so, it was expected of her and her sisters. She wondered briefly what else would be expected. Surely, not much. If they did too much more, they'd be too tired to pay attention in class or even do their homework. And Adele never skipped homework.

It seemed as though they stood there forever waiting for the clothes to finish washing and once they did, a few of the girls ran to the washers and took the clothes out and put them in the huge commercial dryers. They did it almost in synchronization, as if they had done it many, many times and knew exactly how to do it. While it was somewhat fascinating to watch, it was also a little creepy. Their movements were boarding on robotic. Had they been trained? Or brainwashed? Adele remembered a movie she'd watched where a man had implanted chips in people's heads to get them to do what he wanted. While she watched the girls work, her imagination ran away with her and she imagined all the girls having chips in their heads. Then she imagined the next scene where she and her sisters would be led to a cold, dark room to have theirs put in. She made herself shake off the disturbing fantasy and instead concentrated on the girls.

It took another forever for the clothes to dry and once they did, the girls grabbed the clothes, placed them on two long rectangular tables and began folding them at breakneck speed. And they didn't just slap them together, either. They folded them as if they were going to be a display in a store somewhere.

Without question, Adele and her sisters did the same, almost mechanically. It was odd how they just stepped into the roles of laundress laid out for them. It took them a few tries, but by watching how the clothes and sheets and towels were folded, they eventually mimicked the other girls until they got it right. That seemed to take forever and by that time, Adele was ready to sit down and relax. If only. Once this task was done, a good two hours' later, they helped to carry the laundry consisting mainly of the rich girls clothing up the stairs and into their rooms. There were several doors and Adele's group took the first door.

Wow, Adele thought as they entered the rich girls' dormitory. Each girl stayed in an oversized room with another four girls. The beds were beautiful French provincial, each with a little nightstand. The walls were a warm, soft green and were covered with antique artwork. There were several bookshelves scattered here and there laden down with books, stuffed animal and girly knickknacks. There were also small French settees and chairs.

Adele got a little excited. It was exactly the kind of room any girl would have loved to live in. She wondered if her room would be as nice.

She didn't have much time to wonder as she was led to the back of the room where there was a set of double doors which opened up to display a huge closet. There, they put the fresh laundry up and then they went into the massive bathroom and put up the fresh towels.

Once they were done, Ms. Ingles nodded and then turned on her heel. Adele followed her and the other girls out, then waited in the hall until Ms. Ingles inspected every single room. As she would finish, the girls would come out and wait until all the rooms were done. This took roughly over twenty minutes. Finally, they were finished and got into another single line and followed Ms. Ingles down the hall, up a very narrow stairway and into the other girls' room. After all the girls were in, she backed out of the room closing the door behind her and was gone.

After the door closed, Adele turned to the room that she would share with her sisters and all the other girls. As she glanced around at her new sleeping quarters, her heart broke. It literally broke. This was where she and her sisters were going to stay? After seeing the rich girls' rooms, she was devastated by the division of wealth. Not only devastated, but stupefied. Why were they being treated so differently?

The first thing Adele noticed about her room was the long row of twin beds which were so tightly squeezed in together they almost touched. They were each covered in one plain gray cotton blanket and, beneath that, one white sheet. At the top of each bed sat one thin, sad looking pillow.

From the beds, Adele took in the rest of the long, narrow room. It, too, was painted a plain gray color and was totally devoid of any artwork or nice little knickknacks or other personal items from the girls who shared the room. In a word, the room looked tired, so unlike the rest of the house but exactly like the other girls.

"Welcome home," Jane said and threw one arm around Adele's shoulders. "Like it?"

Adele couldn't answer. Of course, she didn't like it, but what difference did that make? More importantly, what choice did she have? This was her new home, if one could call it that and most people wouldn't. No, it was more like an orphanage than a school.

As if reading her thoughts, Jane said, "Yeah, we got the short end of the stick, all us orphaned girls."

"What do you mean?" Adele asked. "We're here on scholarship. Aren't you?"

"Scholarship?" Jane said as laughter erupted from her mouth. "Scholarship? Oh, no, honey, you've been thrown away just like the rest of us."

Almost instinctively, Adele grabbed Cecilia and put her hands over her ears. "Shut up, Jane."

Jane shrugged and gave her a smirk.

"But you're wrong," Adele told her. "Head Mistress Tanner told us that we'd be treated the same as the other girls."

Jane threw her head back and laughed loudly. "Oh, really? Honey, we *are* the other girls."

Adele's mouth dropped and, for a moment, she could not speak. It finally dawned on her. She and her sisters were not on scholarship, probably not even in a school and certainly not an orphanage. What was this place? And why had they ended up here?

Jane removed her arm and nodded once, then flounced away from her and to her own bed, which was almost at the end of the room. Cecilia and Eliza turned to Adele with expectant eyes. They wanted her to tell them it was a lie; that their mother hadn't abandoned them forever, that this wasn't forever. But how could she do that when she didn't know herself?

"She's lying," Adele told them. "Mom will be back soon, just like she promised."

Jane, who must have been waiting and listening, laughed again so the girls could hear her, then called, "Yeah, right, Mountain Girl."

Adele had a sudden urge to sprint across the room and grab Jane and do some bodily harm. But she knew better. She knew not to make trouble, so she held her anger and hostility in.

Just then, a bell went off. The girls snapped to attention and all began putting on their nightgowns, which were stowed under their pillows. Adele watched as they all donned long, gray, thick-cotton gowns. Lotta walked by with her toothbrush and then pointed to three empty beds close to Jane's.

"You can take those beds," she told them. "They've been empty for a while."

"Okay, thanks," Adele said.

"Also, Ms. Ingles left each of you a set of clothes and toothbrushes, too," Lotta said and gave them a small smile.

Adele nodded and she and her sisters went to the beds, found their own nightgowns under the pillows and also a set of clothes which matched the other girls with a pair of worn out mary-jane shoes. There was also a small bar of soap and a set of well-worn towels, along with the toothbrushes.

"It's too big," Cecilia said and held her nightgown up.

"It will be fine," Adele said. "Try it on."

Cecilia shrugged and pulled it over her head. It swamped her. She looked so ridiculous, she got a few chuckles from her sisters. She groaned and pouted. "What am I going to do?"

Adele shrugged. She didn't have any clue. So she said, "Just make do, Cecilia."

Cecilia shrugged then stood back and watched as Adele slipped her nightgown over her head. Once she got it over her head, she wriggled out of her day clothes like she'd seen the other girls do. She wondered if she'd ever have any privacy again. After she made her way into the bathroom to brush her teeth, she knew she wouldn't. The bathroom had only three sinks for all the girls and two small showers and two toilet stalls. The line to use the sinks was long. Adele and her sisters got in line and waited their turns.

Once they were done, they went to their beds, climbed in and it seemed as soon as they got covered up, the lights went out. Just like that. Adele, again, wondered what kind of place this was. She sat up and looked around, staring at all the girls who were covered up and preparing to go to sleep.

None of them made a sound, either. There was no girly chattering or giggling she associated with girls around her age. They were all so exhausted that they immediately fell asleep and Adele was left awake. There was nothing but silence and a slight buzz of the heating unit.

At least we have heat, Adele thought and lay down, closed her eyes and tried to fall asleep. But she couldn't. She sat up again as the ominous feeling came again, the one she'd been having since she'd arrived at Bancroft House. She shook the feeling off and tried not to think about it or about what lay in store for her sisters. She lay back, then squeezed her eyes shut and felt hot, fresh tears on her face. She didn't know if she'd ever been this miserable, even after she'd just found out her father had died.

The Flower Factory

The beautiful bouquet of flowers should have been an indicator of what lay in store for the Clemmons girls. But who would have thought that something so beautiful would inevitably lead to much misery? How could they have known that?

The next day the girls were hustled out of bed at around six-thirty in the morning by Ms. Ingles and then told to brush their teeth, wash their faces and *hurry, hurry, hurry*! Even though it took a while for everyone to get ready, they did so without word and quickly washed faces, brushed teeth and pulled on their gray "school" clothes. Then, as soon as everyone was ready, they followed the woman out of the room. They were led down the hall, down a flight of stairs, to the left, down another hall and then into the rich girls' wing of the house.

Adele stopped outside of a bedroom for a moment and wondered why they were back there so soon, as they'd just been there the previous night. But she soon realized that they were there to make beds, straighten the rooms and wipe down the bathrooms, essentially making them the rich girls' maids. This realization made Adele freeze. It was all a little too surreal. Was this really happening? Was this what was going on? She didn't know and didn't have much time to linger on the thoughts because Jane came up behind her.

"Get to work," she said and gave her a shove.

Adele jumped to it and followed her into the bedroom where she began to make a bed. She glanced over and saw that little Cecilia was having trouble straightening the covers on the bed she was working on. Without a second thought, she walked over and helped her. Then she was abruptly grabbed by the shoulders by Ms. Ingles and shoved towards the bed she was originally making.

"No, she will have to learn how to do it on her own," she said. "Now get back to making this bed."

"But she's too little," Adele said without thinking. "I can do both."

"That's not how it's done here," she snapped. "The girl will learn to make the bed."

Cecilia stared at Adele then at Ms. Ingles, then scrabbled to make the bed, almost having to climb onto it to get the covers right. Adele had a sudden urge to punch the hateful woman in the face but refrained from doing so. She knew it would only lead to trouble and something told her there would soon be much trouble, so it was best to choose her battles wisely.

So, she got to work and helped the others to do their jobs. Once they were finished, they were led down to the dining room. The rich girls had already eaten as was evidenced by the empty bowls of oatmeal and cereal and half-eaten fruit on the table. The other girls jumped into action and cleared their tables and took the dishes into the kitchen where they were put into piles to wash later. Once this task was completed, they made their way back into the dining room and sat down. Three of the girls broke off and went into the kitchen, returning with trays of breakfast food—cold oatmeal, stale toast and a quarter pint of milk.

This has to be the most miserable place on earth, Adele thought to herself as she forced the bland food down. She then made herself smile at Cecilia and at Eliza. When they both returned the smile, Adele vowed to get them all out of there. *There has to be a way out*, she thought. *There has to be.*

Soon, breakfast was over and the girls hurried to clear the tables of the breakfast dishes then were hustled out of the dining room in a single line. Adele breathed a sigh of relief and was actually looking forward to attending class. Anything to take her mind off of the dreadful situation she and her sisters were in would be welcomed relief.

But it was not to be so. The girls didn't go down the hall and into a classroom with a friendly teacher as Adele had anticipated. No, they were instead led down a long, narrow hallway which seemed to stretch for miles and miles and then out into the cold and down a small path and then down a hill. And then Adele saw the building. She recognized it as a conservatory but her gut told her that this wasn't exactly a conservatory. A conservatory was a fancy greenhouse very wealthy people had to grow their own plants and flowers. It was something special and built for the birth and growth of beautiful things and this one rivaled the house in opulence. It was made entirely of brick and glass. The windows had to be at least thirty feet high and the structure was rounded looking so the roof came up to a sharp point and on top of that sharp point sat a beautiful ornate swan weathervane made of cast iron. While the building looked beautiful, Adele got a worrying feeling from it, even though she was in awe of it for a moment. Why were they going to it? Were they going to study botany? Not exactly. Not really. Soon

Adele would find out that inside the conservatory was her and her sister's future. It was a factory. A flower factory, to be exact.

Once they entered, Adele immediately noticed the rows and rows of long, narrow tables. On the tables sat flowers which were being grown in the back of the conservatory. There were mostly roses on the tables, roses that had to be de-stemmed and de-thorned. All colors of roses, all lush and beautiful. All awaiting processing.

Adele figured out what was going on fast. At once she knew what she and her sisters would be doing. She knew they were there to work and the thought tired her. *This is the way it will be for a very long time*, Adele thought and wanted to cry. But she couldn't. She didn't want Eliza or Cecilia to know how much all this was affecting her.

Ms. Ingles watched as all the other girls went to their tables and began to work. As soon as they were busy, she nodded at a petite woman with gray hair who was making her way towards them. Adele stared at her freckled face, then at her denim coveralls and black lace-up boots.

"Hello," she said. "And who do we have here?"

"This is Adele, the oldest, and Eliza and Cecilia," Ms. Ingles told her. "They got in yesterday."

The woman nodded and smiled slightly. She seemed nice, but Adele knew not to trust that.

"This is Sally," Ms. Ingles said. "She oversees the work here. You will listen to her and she will tell you what to do, how to do it and when to do it."

With that, Ms. Ingles turned on her heel and left the conservatory, leaving Adele and her sisters staring after her.

Sally turned to Adele and Eliza. "You two will be working in the back for now. Cecilia will go and work with one of the older girls who will teach her how to package the flowers."

Adele stared at her in disbelief and then asked, "What is this place?"

"No silly questions," she said. "You know what it is. It's a flower factory. And you know what's expected of you. Don't ask me anything else. Just do as you're expected and everything will be fine. Now get to it."

"What about school?" Adele asked against her better judgment.

"I told you not to ask any more silly questions," Sally said, not unkindly. "Now get to work."

So, they got to work. They didn't have a choice. In the back, she and Eliza found the roses, great big thorny bushes of them. They were all overgrown and needed pruning very badly. They looked almost angry. They were a mess.

"How are these things even living?" Eliza asked. "And did you see the amount of roses on the tables? I don't know how these bushes are even producing them."

Adele smiled at her. She talked about flowers just like her mother, just like a grownup. She'd always acted and talked like she was older than she was. Adele patted her back and sighed.

"What do they want us to do with them?" she asked.

"Get them to produce more," Lotta said, coming into the room. "It's been my job for a while but these things are getting out of control. They're going wild."

"I see that," Adele said. "But they're on their last legs. I'm not even sure we can get them back to where they need to be."

Lotta nodded, studying the bushes. She was about to say something when a middle-aged man dressed in chinos and a blue button-down shirt entered the room. When she saw him, she stood up taller and smiled. "Hello, Mr. Adams."

"Good morning, girls," he said and smiled at her, then at Adele and Eliza. "I see you've got some new helpers."

"I do," Lotta said.

He nodded, then turned to Adele. "Well, I've certainly heard a lot about you, Adele."

"You have?" she asked in bewilderment. Who was this man? And how did he already know her name? Maybe Head Mistress Tanner had told him about her. She didn't know, but she did get a creepy feeling from it.

"Yes, you and you sister," he said, giving one nod to Eliza. "You don't remember me, do you?"

Adele and Eliza glanced sideways at each other before turning back to him and shaking their heads. But then... Something stirred in the back of her mind about the man. She did recognize him but couldn't remember from where. *Who was he?* Then something came to her. She vaguely remembered a man stopping by the house and getting out of a fancy car a few years ago during the summer. He had been astounded at their flower garden.

"Oh, the girls did that," her mother had told him, laughing. This was only partially true. They did help plant and prune and water the flowers, but it was her that did most of the work. Of course, she had instilled the importance of flowers, of beautiful things in each of the girls. She would tell them to take time and not only smell the roses but to pick them as well. She would tell them never to overlook the value in doing something for beauty's sake.

"You girls have green thumbs," he said. "And that's why I need you to help me out with something."

He walked over to a door Adele hadn't noticed and motioned them over to him. When they were at his side, he opened the door and they walked in. Inside the small room were hundreds of small pitiful potted plants with long stems growing out the top of them. They looked almost dead.

"They're orchids," he said. "And they need help. They won't grow. They're not blooming as they should."

Eliza went over to one and studied it. She pushed her finger down into the soil and shook her head. "You're overwatering them. They're dying."

The man jerked back and nodded once.

"I've read about orchids," Eliza said. "They're very fragile and need constant care."

"What do you suggest?" he asked her.

She shrugged. "I read that you can't water them. You have to place ice cubes on top of the soil about once a week. They take a lot of what they need from the air and the air in here is really too cold. They like swamps. They like to be hot. They'll never do well here."

The man nodded. "So we just need to get some ice cubes and some heat?"

"Pretty much," Eliza said.

"Can you two girls help me bring these back?" he asked. "I've invested quite a bit of money and time into these things."

Adele stared at him. And what would she be getting out of it? She didn't like any of this and she particularly didn't like knowing this man once came to her house and now they were suddenly here, in his conservatory—or flower factory, rather. It was almost like they were brought here to work for him. And Adele resented that.

"Sure, we can help," Eliza said.

Adele wanted to pinch her. What about school? What about something besides all this work? What were they doing here, anyway? None of it added up and none of it made sense and she knew it wouldn't for a very long time.

"Great!" he said and clapped his hands together once. "I'll see about pumping in some more heat and getting some ice. Thanks, girls."

And with that, he disappeared out the door. Adele and Eliza looked at each other, not knowing what to do.

Lotta poked her head in and said, "Come back out here and help me. He won't be back today or probably for a long while. He's been trying to get those orchids to do something for a while now. I think he's a little obsessed."

"Who is he?" Adele asked her.

"He owns the school," she said.

"You mean the prison?"

Lotta laughed. "It certainly seems like that, doesn't it? But, anyway, I heard he inherited it from his father, so it's been around for a while. You know, it's not that bad. You just have to suck it up. We'll be old enough to leave soon. That's what I'm counting on anyway."

Adele didn't comment. She and Eliza went back to the rose bushes and began to work with them. Soon enough, their hands were covered in scratches, which reminded her of the scratches her mother used to get when she worked with her rose bushes. She turned to Lotta.

"Hey, Lotta," she said. "I was wondering when I would be able to call my mom."

"Your mom?" she asked.

"Yeah," she said. "I'd like to talk to her, see if she got home okay and everything."

Lotta just stared at her. "Adele, I don't think they let you do that."

Adele's mouth dropped. "What?"

Lotta sighed and leaned back a little to stare at her. "I mean, you could ask the head mistress, but she usually doesn't allow any outside contact unless, of course, the parents contact you."

"You mean I can't call her?"

She nodded, then stopped. "I mean no."

"What if I just snuck into her office and did it?" Adele asked.

"She'd know when she saw the phone bill," Lotta replied and gave her a look of concern. "Adele, just don't, okay? You could get into some major trouble if you did something like that. If you even ask to do something like that, you get on their radar. You don't ever want to be on their radar."

Adele wasn't sure what she meant, but knew that if she couldn't even talk to her mother, how would she survive this place?

"Just wait for her to call you," Lotta said.

"But what if she doesn't?"

"She'll call, I'm sure," Lotta said. "Or send a letter."

Adele nodded and got back to work, deciding that she'd have to find a way to be okay with all this. But how was she supposed to be okay with not talking to her own mother? She didn't know how, she'd just have to figure it out. She'd put her mind on other things, like school. That made her pause for a minute and she asked Lotta, "So, when do we go to school?"

"Oh, once a day," Lotta said. "Between three and five, then we go to dinner."

"What?" Eliza asked. "We only go two hours a day?"

Lotta nodded. "Ms. Tanner says that everything you need to learn you can learn in that length of time."

"Is she serious?" Adele asked. "What about graduating and going to college?"

She shrugged. "I dunno. All I know is that we go to class for two hours a day."

Adele's heart sank. Knowing that she wouldn't be going to class killed her as much as just being at this place. She'd always loved school, loved learning and had big plans on being a teacher, maybe even a professor in a college. Now what? Now she was nothing more than a maid and a gardener for some strange man. It didn't add up, none of it. When would it start making sense? She knew she was in for a long, hard row and she did not look forward to it.

The girls soon settled into a routine. They were up around six-thirty, awakened by Ms. Ingles, then they got ready for the day. Then down to the rich girls' rooms to straighten and clean up. Then breakfast, then work in the flower factory with Sally who constantly rode them to work harder, harder, harder! Around noon, they were served plain brown paper bag lunches which usually consisted of a few carrots, a soggy peanut butter and jelly sandwich and a small carton of milk. Then work until three and then two hours of class in which all the girls were crammed into a large room with no desks and only a few ratty old books which they all shared.

The girls were split up into three groups based on their age. Their teacher, a middle-aged woman with a tight bun and a hateful face, taught them from a chalkboard. She insisted they call her Professor Wheaton, though it was obvious she wasn't a real professor and Adele even doubted she had a college degree. They basically skimmed lessons in history, math and reading. Anytime anyone had a question, she would become flustered and shake her head and tell them something like, "Don't worry about that. Just stick to the book." The woman could barely answer the basic questions on long division!

The lessons were so short and basic, Adele began to worry that Cecelia wouldn't learn anything. She began to tutor her on the side during their "free" time, which was about thirty minutes each day before they went to sleep at night. It really worried her that none of them were going to get an education and poor, little Cecelia might not even learn how to properly read and write. She could read some and write some, but because she was so young she needed special attention. Adele did the best she could but by the time they got a break to work together, Cecelia was exhausted and wanted to rest. She hated their lessons and would rail whenever Adele brought them up. But Adele persisted and wouldn't let her off the hook. If nothing else, she *had* to read and write.

After their lessons, the girls went into the dining room and sat at their table. A few of them, on a rotating schedule, went into the kitchen and helped get supper prepared while the others waited. Once it was ready, the rich girls were served, then the other girls. The dinners were hushed affairs for the other girls and they would steal glances at the rich girls who were, for all intents and purposes, having the time of their lives. It wasn't lost on Adele that if someone had entered the school and only observed the rich girls, they would have thought this place was the bee's knees.

It was far from that for the other girls. After dinner, it was clean up time, then onto laundry, sometimes dusting of the classrooms or mopping of the floors. There was always so much to do that by the time they got to their room at night, they were ready to collapse and usually did.

Though they were constantly busy, time moved very slowly. It was if it took weeks for a day to be done. And a week was like a month. The whole time-frame at the school was like a long winter day where you had nothing to do and couldn't get out of the house. It was like they were all standing at a window, staring out at the dull gray sky and wondering if it would ever change to a brilliant blue.

It never did.

Though the Clemmons girls didn't learn much in the way of school, they did learn many other things at Bancroft House. They learned if they showed any emotions, they would be taunted for them. If they showed anger, they would get beatings from the teacher/superiors. "Just keep quiet, do your job and go on," Lotta told her one day after another other girl was paddled outside the conservatory for refusing to work and yelling at Sally. Though none of them had actually seen the paddling, they had heard the girls' wails. It was not only too much for Adele, but too much for her sisters, who looked wide-eyed at her while it was happening. But what could she do? The feeling of being out of control was almost unbearable. So, she took Lotta's advice and just kept quiet. That was the best course of action, so she and her sisters learned that they that they had to stop processing their emotions in order to stay out of trouble.

They learned that fear was met with anger. Anger was met with more anger. Sadness was met with ridicule. Love? The only love they felt was for one another and they learned quickly to hide it so no one could take it away from them. Their love was what bonded them and kept them from slipping into too great of a depression.

As they days passed, the girls simply accepted their fate. Adele tried to fantasize about the day when their mother might return. She *had* promised but as days turned into weeks and weeks turned into months, she knew, in her heart she *knew*, that her mother wasn't coming anytime soon, if ever. She tried to ignore the fact that her mother hadn't called them or sent any letters. Adele tried to reassure herself that she would eventually when she got time. She was probably busy with a new job and saving money to come rescue them. Adele made herself believe that because if she had no hope of anything ever getting better, what was the use? Without hope, nothing would be worth anything.

Of course, the thought that she and her sisters had really been abandoned so soon after losing their father was constantly in the back of her mind. Surely her mother hadn't abandoned them. Surely not. But as the days stretched on with no calls and no letters, Adele was beginning to forget what it felt like to hope for her mother's return. But she couldn't allow herself to dwell on it. She had to keep some hope.

So, with no other recourse, Adele hunched her shoulders and did her work. She loosely befriended some of the other girls, but mostly kept her distance. She just didn't trust anyone. She didn't want to be their friends because that meant this was permanent and if that were true, she knew she'd sink into an awful sadness from which she might not ever recover.

But the hardest work to be done was in the flower factory. Those hours were long and hard. Adele sometimes thought that she would rather work in the coal mines of West Virginia like her father than do this. She and Eliza were assigned to bring back the orchids and then splitting the plants to make new orchids. It was tedious work, as the flowers were so delicate they'd snap in two if you looked at them the wrong way. But they did it and soon the flowers began to grow and flourish. She knew the flowers were being sold, just how was a mystery. She liked to imagine to a local flower shop, but she had an idea that they were being sent all over the world, probably through a website of some sort.

Once the orchids were under control, she and Eliza, along with Lotta, got to work on the rose bushes and they were a bear. It was almost as if the things were rebelling and throwing out their thorns to keep them away. It was probably just from years and years of usage and the bushes were tired. Newer ones had to be planted to take the place of the older, more stubborn ones and, in the meanwhile, the older ones had to be brought under control. This took weeks but soon, just like they had with the orchids, they were able to get them producing healthier, prettier looking roses. Sally was quite impressed with their work and even congratulated them on it.

While Adele appreciated the compliment, she questioned Sally's authority, if only to herself. Didn't she know that you couldn't let a rose bush go like that? It would grow wild, like these had. Soon she realized the woman was just supervising the girls and really didn't know that much about the flowers. She had left them to grow on their own and you couldn't do that with roses. You had to tend to them, baby them and pray they'd produce. Adele knew this and she wasn't even fifteen years old yet. She realized that if she and Eliza hadn't come along, the roses would have stopped producing altogether and the flower factory shut down. Adele really hated this. If she and her sisters hadn't arrived at Bancroft House, the other girls might have had an easier life after a while.

Mr. Adams was overjoyed with the results, as well. "I can't believe you girls did it!" he exclaimed and clapped his hands together. "How wonderful!"

It was wonderful but he didn't see the amount of work that had gone into getting those flowers producing. And he probably didn't care much, either.

But Adele tried not to let it bother her. She simply went on with her work and tried to think of the day when she could get herself and her sisters out of that miserable place. She accepted her fate for the time being, kept her head down, her mouth shut and her eyes peeled for opportunities. However, opportunities are hard to come by and even when they do, people rarely recognize them for the gifts they are. But right then, Adele just concentrated on getting through the day, just like she was today.

It was after noon when her stomach grumbled. She looked up at the clock, then turned to Sally, who was walking between the rows of tables inspecting the girls' work. Adele was out helping process roses that day because all her other work was under control. She and Eliza and Lotta did that. They'd do their work with the bushes and the orchids, then come into the processing room and help remove thorns from the roses and pack the orchids into boxes to be shipped out. It seemed as though they never stopped working. Even lunch was a hurried affair.

Just as Sally passed her, Adele turned to her and asked, "Isn't it time for lunch?" she asked.

"No lunch today," she said. "Your cook is out sick."

"What do you mean no lunch?" Adele asked, almost in a panic.

"No lunch means no food," she said. "They're trying to call someone in so you girls can get some supper, but they won't be here before three. Now get back to work."

Adele stared at her in pain. No food meant being weak. She was so sick of being weak. Great. Not only was it another long day, it was another long day with no food. How she and the other girls kept going on what they were fed was a miracle.

She almost started crying in frustration, but then glanced over at Cecelia and stopped. She refused to break down in front of her. It wasn't fair to the little girl to be in such turmoil all the time. The only normalcy she had in her life was the fact that her older sisters could keep it together. If they couldn't at least do that, then what would happen to her?

The day dragged on and on. It seemed to take forever before they went to their lesson and then that dragged on and on. All their stomachs were in knots from hunger and as soon as they were able to go into the dining room, they all breathed a sigh of relief in unison.

Adele sat down and waited, then noticed Jane pointing at the kitchen. "What?" she asked her.

"It's your turn tonight, Mountain Girl," Jane said, rolling her eyes. "Let's get to it."

Adele suddenly felt deflated, even defeated. Since she had to serve, she wouldn't be allowed to eat until *after* every one else was served. But she didn't fight it. She simply got up and followed Jane into the kitchen there she helped prepare the rich girls' food first. Their meal tonight was a small, sirloin steak, a baked potato with creamy and delicious smelling butter and a side of asparagus covered with a white, creamy hollandaise sauce. Adele knew all this because she had served this meal many times and each time she served it, it was all she could do not to take a piece of the delicious meat and cram it into her mouth.

After she had loaded down her serving tray, she went out into the dining room and began to serve. As she took the plates off the tray and sat them down, she ignored the rich girls, as they ignored her. There was no "please" or "thank you" or anything like that. It was as if the other girls were elves who came in, served, then left. It was almost as if they were completely and totally invisible.

But something was off today. In fact, it had been off every day that Adele served. There was one girl in particular who always gave her looks, looks that made her feel intimidated and like she didn't belong. At least that's the way she felt. She knew the rich girls basically ignored the other girls, but this girl had made a point of not ignoring Adele. In fact, she acted like she had something against her. This would come off as smirks and Adele knew the girl really looked down on her. She hated serving her, but she had to do it. If she didn't serve, she'd have no supper. And the girl was waiting on her, waiting for her to serve her. She felt dread fill her body. She felt so low, almost subhuman. She avoided the girl's eyes but felt them on her, watching her every move.

Adele glanced up and hoped that Jane would reach the girl before she did. Of course, she was on the far end of the table serving and didn't even cast a look in her direction. *Great*, Adele thought. *Just great.* She was nearing her chair and she glanced down at her tray, hoping she'd run out of plates before she reached her. Of course, she was down to her last plate when she came to the girl. Instinct told her to take it back to the kitchen and pretend she was out of food. But she ignored the instinct, instead hoping to just get it over, serve the girl, get done and eat her meal.

As she sat the plate down, the girl moved back and curled her lips. Adele noticed she had thick auburn hair and deep brown eyes. Her face was very white, pasty even. She was pretty, but Adele knew she was prettier. And the girl knew it, too.

"That'll be all, girl," the girl said, smirking.

What? Adele stared at her in bewilderment as squeals of laughter erupted from around the table. She heard some of the rich girls whispering about this girl who had now deigned to speak to her, to Adele, who was one of the lowly other girls. She was obviously the alpha-female of the group. That meant she had power over all the rich girls. That meant she could get away with almost anything.

Adele grew very embarrassed, so embarrassed that her face flushed so quickly she could feel the heat. She knew she should ignore the comment and she knew she should walk away as quickly as she could and never look back but she was frozen. Something in her refused to be cowed down by this girl. It might have been the fact that she was, in fact, a mountain girl. It might have been the fact that she'd taken so much since she'd been at Bancroft house she was about to burst at the seams. Or it might have been the fact that this girl really, really rubbed her the wrong way. Not only that, the little snob was now trying to embarrass her. Couldn't she see Adele was subordinate to her? And that, perhaps, nothing she could say or do to Adele would make her any more inferior than she already felt?

But Adele was wrong. There was something the girl could do to make her feel even worse about her situation. And she did it. Just as soon as Adele determined the best course of action was to walk away and ignore her, the girl took action. She wasn't about to let it go. She thrust out her leg and Adele tripped and fell right on her face. She hit so hard she saw stars and a flash of black and almost passed out. It was probably from the hunger, she realized. But her hunger was the least of her worries right then. The empty tray went flying out in front of her and skidded across the floor. Adele heard the rich girl's laughter as she fell, as she went down in pain and humiliation. But as soon as she hit the floor, something took over her and in an instant she was back up and had slapped the girl across the face before she could stop herself. Everyone gasped and the girl withdrew in horror. Adele did, too, as she knew what she'd just done would cost her dearly.

The whole room stopped eating, talking, doing whatever it was they were doing and they turned to Adele and the rich girl. Mouths dropped as were forks and spoons. Something like this never happened. One of the other girls never crossed a rich girl. It was just not done. And to actually hit a one? Oh, brother. That was something they never even spoke of. Adele knew she was in for it and, when she glanced across the room, her eyes met those of Head Mistress Tanner, who was just coming in to check on things. The head mistress, who had seen everything, was not happy. In six long strides, she was over to Adele. Adele immediately turned to run out of instinct, but the head mistress grabbed her before she could make a move. She pulled her from the room, almost throwing her out the door.

Once they were in the hall, she turned to her and nearly growled, "Do you know who you just hit?"

Adele didn't.

"That girl's father owns a banking corporation and…" She stopped, so furious she couldn't even go on. "If he knew something like this happened to his child, he would have my head!"

There was no way that Adele could have known this. She and the other girls were so separated from the rich girls they didn't even know their names.

"I don't know what to do with you just yet," she said. "Go to your room and stay there until I send for you."

"But I haven't eaten," Adele said, almost crying. "I haven't eaten all day. We didn't get lunch and—"

"Well, I guess you should have thought about that when you slapped her, shouldn't you?"

"She tripped me!" Adele cried, tears streaming down her cheeks. "She—

"Shut up and go!" she roared and pointed to the stairs.

Adele knew it was pointless to argue. You couldn't argue and expect to win a fight with someone who barely considered you to be a human. Whatever you said to them would be misconstrued and turned against you. Adele knew she was beaten and she knew she would do without any supper. With no other recourse, she went to her room. Once there, she just laid down on her bed and cried. She wanted to stop but couldn't make herself. The only upside was that she didn't have to do any chores that night.

Soon enough, the other girls started coming into the room. They mostly ignored her except for Eliza who sat down beside her, gave her a quick hug and hurried off to her bed. She was never a big talker, never showed too much emotion but Adele knew how much she loved her. It was comforting to know someone did but it didn't do much to take any of the pain away.

Adele pushed her head into her pillow for a moment, then looked up to see Lotta staring at her. She stared at her, wondering what she wanted.

"Told you they were trouble," she said. "The rich girls. I told you."

Adele didn't answer and wished she'd go away.

"You shouldn't have hit her," she said, giving her a stern look.

"What I was I supposed to do?" Adele asked in frustration.

"Take it," Lotta replied.

But Adele was sick of taking it. She'd taken it since she'd gotten to Bancroft House. She'd kept her mouth shut, allowed these people to treat her and her sisters like dirt and she'd just snapped when the girl tripped her. The awful thing about it was that she didn't even know the girl's name, let alone her motivation. But, yes, she had to agree she should have let the girl humiliate her and continued on her way. Now she was paying the price and she hoped that this would be all she would have to pay.

But was it ever going to get any better? Soon, it would be her birthday and then Cecelia's and then Eliza's. She knew there would be no special treatment for them, let alone a birthday cake. And what about Thanksgiving and Christmas? The start of the holiday season was only a few weeks or so away. She knew they'd be spending the holidays here and there would be no Christmas gifts or a turkey. For some reason, this really bothered her. She hated thinking about how her life, and the lives of her sisters, was slowly grinding to a halt, all in tribute to waiting hand and foot on a bunch of snobs. It was never going to be about her or Eliza or Cecelia. It was all going to be about them—the rich girls and the flowers. And once they turned on her, as the girl had done today, life would be made even harder and more unbearable. She didn't know how much more she could take.

"Just go away, Lotta," Adele said and pushed her face into her pillow.

Lotta stared at her for a moment, then left, leaving Adele to stew. Soon, Cecelia came over to give her a good night hug and a good night kiss.

"I'm sorry, sissy," she whispered in her little voice.

"It's okay," Adele said. "I wasn't hungry anyway."

Cecelia tried to smile and then raced to her bed and got in, covered herself up and closed her eyes. Adele stared at her and wondered how long they were going to be in this miserable hellhole. She didn't know but she did know she couldn't take much more.

Not long after that, the lights went off and everyone settled in. Adele tried to go to sleep but kept tossing and turning. She didn't know how long she did that, but it seemed like forever. The hunger was keeping her awake. She tried to close her eyes and count sheep, but the hunger pangs wouldn't let her.

She sat up on her elbows and looked around the room. All the other girls were fast asleep and if they weren't, they weren't paying any attention to her. She could not go another minute without something to eat. It was that bad.

She thought about it for a moment before gaining the confidence to go through with it. She'd never left the room at night and wasn't sure if there was anyone on night watch or not. If there was, she could get in trouble. If there wasn't, she might be able to find something to eat. As her stomach let out an enormous growl, she decided to risk it.

Quietly, she threw the covers back and swung her legs over the edge of the bed. Her feet hit the cold, hard floor and almost ached in pain. But the pain of hunger was greater, so she carried on.

She got up quickly and padded out of the room, not looking back. She stole through the door and out into the hallway, taking her time to be as quiet as a church mouse. She breathed a sigh of relief when she didn't see anyone as she made her way towards the kitchen. The entire house was quiet and, as she passed a big grandfather clock, it clanged, announcing midnight. She almost jumped out of her skin, but then regained her composure and crept silently down the stairs, to the left and through the dining room and into the vast kitchen.

She paused at the door and looked around. She hurried across the floor, opened the refrigerator, peered in and became overwhelmed at all the food in there. There was thick cut bacon and fresh eggs for breakfast and cold cuts for sandwiches for lunch. For supper there were stacks of small, petite steaks and lots of fresh vegetables. It was food for the rich girls, she realized, and not for the other girls. She was tired of doing without but indignity almost made her slam the door and retreat to her room. *How dare they keep us from eating well?* But something caught her eye. It was pudding, dark chocolate pudding. She hadn't had any pudding in months, maybe even for a year, and it was her favorite desert. She'd seen the rich girls feast on it before but never thought she'd have the opportunity to do the same. There were about five or so small white ramekins of pudding left.

Without thinking, she grabbed the ramekin of pudding, shut the refrigerator door and looked around for a spoon. She walked quickly to the cabinets, opened a drawer and found one. Then she dipped the spoon in and brought it to her mouth. Once the rich, sweet, chocolate goodness reached her taste-buds, Adele was almost in heaven. It had been too long since she'd eaten chocolate and this pudding was some of the best she'd ever had.

"What are doing?"

Startled, Adele looked up to see Jane staring at her. Jane sighed, shook her head and went over to the drawer to retrieve her own spoon. She walked over to Adele, dipped her spoon in and took a big bite of the pudding.

"I thought I was the only one who did this, Mountain Girl," she said with a wicked grin.

"You do this?" Adele asked and wondered why she hadn't thought of doing it before now.

"Always have," Jane said and took another bite. "You can't survive on what they feed you. It's a wonder the girls don't start dropping off."

"I know," Adele agreed.

"But you have to be careful," she said. "If they find out we're breaking the rules, there will be hell to pay."

Adele nodded and took another bite of the pudding, wishing Jane would go away and let her have it all. As if she'd read her mind, Jane stopped and turned on her heel, winked at her from over her shoulder and made her way into the pantry. Adele couldn't help but follow her.

Once there, Jane opened up her arms and said, "The motherlode."

Adele peered in to see the overstuffed shelves full of good, rich food. And all they got was stupid beans and beans and sometimes rice! There was tea and soda and loaves of fresh-baked breads and even croissants! Adele had once had a croissant when she'd begged for one in the grocery store back home. She loved its buttery taste and the flakiness of it. She grinned and grabbed one and took a big bite. Oh, it was heaven, almost as good as the pudding. She chewed it and swallowed and went in for another bite.

Jane chuckled to herself and grabbed and piece of bread then some peanut butter and, with the spoon she'd been eating with, made herself a sandwich. She took a bite, chewed and stared at Adele.

"You know, we're a lot alike," she said.

"We are?" Adele asked and had to make herself refrain from rolling her eyes. She knew that she and Jane were nothing alike and that all they had in common was hunger.

"Yeah," she said. "We're smarter than all these other people."

"I guess," Adele said and finished the croissant and then grabbed the peanut butter and took a big bite, which gave her instant pleasure and satisfaction. "That is so good!"

Jane laughed a little and shook her head. "You really got that girl good today."

Adele nodded. "I guess I did."

"Sometimes they do that," she said. "A new girl will come in and because she might be prettier than they are, they get a little jealous. That's why she taunted you, you know?"

Adele didn't know. She just thought he was being mean. But then it all made sense. Why else would you want to pick on someone if you weren't threatened by them? What was the fun in that? There was no real challenge.

"And they do it to their own kind, too," Jane said. "Even new rich girls get a little bullying."

"Have they done it to you?" Adele asked.

Jane shook her head. "Look at me. I'm almost six-foot tall. I'm skinny but I am strong. Why would those little mean girls mess with me?"

She had a point.

"That's why I have to come down here and eat," she continued. "I'm so tall that if I didn't, I wouldn't be able to get out of bed and work those damned flowers."

Adele almost laughed, thinking about the absurdity of it all. "How do they get away with it?" she asked. "I mean, look at what they make us do. Isn't there a law against that?"

"Well, there probably is," Jane said. "But we are in school a couple hours a day and they could say the flowers are some sort of recreation or that we're on work study. Who knows how they get away with it? And no one probably cares, that's the real kicker. I mean, we're basically all orphans, aren't we? If we weren't here, we'd be in another system somewhere that might even be worse."

Adele thought about that. What could be worse than this? Then she realized that Jane was right. This was bad, but other things could be even shoddier.

"What happened to your parents?" Adele asked her.

She sighed with a touch of sadness and said, "Drugs. Yours?"

"My father died working in the coal mines," she told her. "And my mother couldn't take care of us."

"So, you mother is still alive?" she asked.

Adele nodded.

"Huh," she said but didn't go any further. "Listen, the trick is to just ride it out. That's right. And once you hit eighteen, you're free."

"Free to do what?" Adele asked.

"To do anything you want," Jane said. "I've got two more years and after that, I am gone. I don't know what I'm going to do or where I'm going, but I'm out of here. And they can't bring me back, either."

"What do you mean—bring you back?"

"I ran away once," she said. "Or twice or maybe three times. But they always found me and brought me back."

"Why did you run away?"

"Isn't it obvious, Mountain Girl?" she asked with a laugh. "This place sucks. God! Are you serious? I mean, what girl would want to be the maid of some snooty rich girls and then the worker bee of a flower factory and then, on top of that, be starved? We're young. We're supposed to be thinking about prom and babysitting jobs and new clothes and, God forbid—boyfriends! What about college? Isn't that what girls our age are supposed to be thinking about? Yeah, but we're not, are we? What do we have to look forward to? It ain't ever Christmas here for a reason."

Adele felt a sinking feeling in her stomach. It was true. They were never going to get out, not until they were eighteen. Maybe if she could hang on until she turned eighteen, she could get a job and get her sisters and they could all live together. She liked that idea. But that was more than three years away. She didn't know if she could stand it that long.

Jane stared at her, then sighed. "I didn't mean to bring you down. I know how hard it is here. It's just the thought of leaving and never having to come back to this hellhole makes me a little crazy. I just want to leave so bad."

"Maybe it's not that bad," Adele said.

"It *is* that bad," Jane said. "But you just have to learn to live with it. Like I do. You don't have a choice otherwise." She finished the sandwich off and then screwed the lid back on the peanut butter. "We better get going."

Adele nodded and watched as she put the peanut butter back in the exact place she'd found it, then arranged the bread so that it looked like none was missing. She took the ramekin of pudding out of Adele's hand and stared at it, shaking her head.

"We'll have to wash this," she said. "We ate it all."

"Okay," Adele said.

"The trick is to make it look like nothing is missing," she said. "Only eat a little at a time. Remember that next time. You understand?"

Adele nodded.

"Never take more than you need," she said. "If they found out we were doing this, there would be a high price to pay."

"Okay," Adele said.

"Also, we both can't come down here at the same time," she said. "We have to keep it separate. I'll come first, right at midnight and you can come an hour later. Just wait for me to get back to the room. Got it?"

Adele wondered if she could trust what she was saying. She decided she could—with caution—so she nodded in agreement.

Jane walked out of the pantry, leaving Adele to make sure nothing looked out of place. As she did so, she heard Jane quickly washing the ramekin and putting it into a cupboard. Then she heard her take two steps, then nothing.

She paused and waited, wondering what Jane was doing. She went to the door, opened it and, to her utter shock, saw Head Mistress Tanner standing in front of Jane. She looked around Jane's shoulder at Adele and her thin lips formed two hard lines.

"Get over here, Adele," Head Mistress Tanner said.

Adele had no choice. She went over, head down, and stood beside Jane. Adele noticed that Jane was very nervous and thought about how articulate and self-possessed she'd been just a few minutes earlier. Now she was reduced to shaking like a leaf on a tree, one in a very bad storm.

"What are you two doing in here?" she snapped. When neither of them answered, she snapped, "Answer me!"

"She got up and I followed her out," Jane said hurriedly. "I was going to report her to you."

Adele's mouth dropped and she stood there, stupefied. She couldn't believe she'd just been sold out! And here she thought they'd bonded and were becoming friends. She'd been right about Jane all along. You couldn't trust someone like her. Her first impression was correct, as first impressions usually are. Jane was untrustworthy.

"Is that true, Adele?" Head Mistress Tanner asked.

Adele glanced at Jane, who stood there frightened. She realized she was stronger than her. She realized Jane was nothing more than what her mother would call a blow-hard—all talk and no walk. She knew she could take the heat but the heat would kill someone so weak like Jane. And she was no snitch.

"It is," Adele said.

Jane's mouth dropped at her words. Adele refused to look at her again. She was finished with her. This would be the end of any friendship.

"Back to bed, Jane," the head mistress told her then pointed at Adele. "You come with me."

Jane scampered out of the room and Adele followed Head Mistress Tanner back to her office. She was told to stand beside her desk and wait. And she did so, watching as the head mistress opened a drawer filled with all sorts of candy. Adele recognized her favorite candy bar and for an instant longed to grab it, rip open the wrapper and devour it. She would have been willing to accept whatever punishment there was just for a taste. However, it was obviously the wrong drawer and the head mistress grunted slightly, then slammed the drawer shut before going on to the next one where she rummaged around and then pulled out a small but thick piece of oak cut into a paddle shape. Adele knew what it was and what it was used for. An image of the other girl who'd been paddled came back to her. She winced, knowing what she was in store for. She only hoped she was wrong about.

"Hold out your hands," Head Mistress Tanner said.

Adele's eyes widened. Was she really going to hit her? On her hands?

"Now," she demanded.

Adele didn't have much choice. She held her hands out, palms facing up and watched in horror as the head mistress brought the paddle down across her palms. Pain shot through her and made her nauseous for a moment. She thought she might even pass out. It hurt that much. But it wasn't over. She gave her another four whacks and then put the paddle up.

Adele stood there for a long moment willing her hands to stop throbbing with pain. She couldn't move as another wave of nausea came over her.

"Now that is for the slap earlier today and for the thievery," she said. "Now get yourself into bed and wake up tomorrow with a better attitude or else."

Adele couldn't let that go. Even though she was in a lot of pain and should have learned her lesson, she had to say, "Or else what?"

"You don't want to find out."

"Maybe I do."

"Girl," she said, almost growling. "You don't want to cause any more disruption. You don't know who you're dealing with."

Oh, she did. She had an idea of who—and what—she was dealing with. She knew all about this woman just by looking at her. She knew how mean she was. Adele wouldn't confront her on it, but she knew about her. And she liked to think the head mistress knew that she knew, too.

"You're dismissed," Head Mistress Tanner told her and gave a wave of hand.

Adele wasn't about to let it go that easily. She wanted this woman to know that she knew all about her. And she wanted to provoke her enough to do her more bodily harm. If she did that, Adele might just get sent to a hospital and in that hospital she might be able to get the ear of a sympathetic nurse or doctor. She was done being told what to do, when to do it and being starved on top of it. She was from the mountains and mountain girls didn't take too much before giving some of it back.

Adele turned to her and said, very matter-of-factly, "You lied to my mother. You told her we were going to school. You said we were here on scholarship. What scholarship? We don't even get to attend class."

She laughed harshly. "Your mother sold you and your sisters to me. I intend to recoup my investment."

"What are you talking about?"

"You don't get it, do you?" she asked. "You were not brought here on scholarship. There is no scholarship! You were brought here to work. Your mother sold you to the school. She was broke and about to lose everything. She made the call, I told her what I could give her and the next thing I know, she's here with you three girls. That means that I am now your legal guardian."

"You liar!" Adele yelled. "You lied to her! You tricked her, that's all!"

"Believe me, I did no such thing and it didn't take that much convincing or that much money, either." She paused and glared at Adele. "And, no, I'm not lying," she said. "Your mother was desperate. Did you know how sick she was? She didn't have a choice."

"Sick?" Adele asked. "She wasn't sick."

She smiled at her knowingly. "Oops. Now get yourself back upstairs, into bed and be prepared for a full work load tomorrow."

"My mother was not sick," Adele said. "You're just saying that to make me mad, that's all."

"Why else would she drop you and your sisters off here?" she asked. "Why else would a perfectly healthy woman give her three children up? She just dropped you off, didn't she? And she never calls or sends letter. Wonder why?"

Adele stared at her, her mouth open. She had to be lying. She *had* to be. What if she was right? What if her mother was sick? Oh, God, what if she died and Adele and her sisters didn't even know it? But was this real? Or was it a scare tactic? And if was, how would she ever know? It was too much.

"Back to bed," she said.

Adele didn't say another word. The old woman had gotten her. She turned on her heel and exited the room without another word. Once she was outside and had the door shut, she leaned on it, not knowing what to do. She wanted to run away so bad she couldn't stand it. But where could she go? How far would her weak body take her?

She stared down at her hands, which were throbbing with pain. She shook them and then became overwhelmed with emotion. Not knowing what to do, she just started running and found herself running through the halls, looking for a way out. She was having trouble breathing and needed to find a place where she could be alone and break down and cry. She knew she was in for a storm of tears and had to be somewhere alone to let them out. She kept running and looking, searching for a place to break down but it seemed as though the halls opened up to more halls. She got to one of them and finally found a door at the end. She opened it then saw a staircase leading down into the basement. She hadn't even known there was a basement.

Without thinking, she stepped in, shut the door and raced down the stairs. Once she got the last step, she took a moment to look around. The room was quite large and there were rows and rows of shelves stuffed with old dusty holiday decorations and toys. There were old pots and pans from the kitchen but mostly just an enormous amount of junk. Adele didn't care. She looked around for a corner where she could hide and get her emotions out. She raced between the rows of shelves and came to the end of room and there was yet another door. She paused for a moment before opening it, then went through it.

It was just a closet. The bare concrete floor was dirty and there were mops that smelled of bleach and old tin buckets. She pushed some of the junk to the side and slid down the wall, pulling her knees into her chest and putting her head on her knees. Then she started crying. She stayed like that until the sobs subsided and that was probably a good ten minutes.

Of course, when the crying stopped, she felt like a fool. What had she been thinking? She knew the rules. You were not supposed to leave your room after lights out and, more importantly, you were not supposed to steal food. But the hunger forced her into survival mode and within that there was no reason.

But what about her mother? What if she was really sick? What if something had happened to her? The head mistress was right. There had been no phone calls or letters. Not a word since they'd parted that day. She had to be sick; she might even be dead. Fresh tears stung her eyes and she sobbed thinking of all the awful things her mother might be experiencing right now.

If only she could get out of there. If only she could gather her two sisters up and leave. If only they could leave and find their mother, they could help her, nurse her back to health. Her being sick was the only obvious explanation of why she had left them in such a horrible circumstance. *I have to get out of here*, she kept thinking, almost chanting to herself over and over. *I have to leave, I have to do it*. She wanted to get away from Bancroft House so badly she couldn't think straight. All she could think of was leaving, escaping. She didn't care what she had to do to get out of that place, where she had to go, what she had to do. But how?

But there was no way. There was no way out. She was stuck. She was too young and, not only that, her sisters were too young, too. If they left, she was sure they'd be brought right back. And then more punishment and more pain. No, she had no choice. She had to stay and protect her sisters. If she could leave on her own, she might be able to make it work but the thought of being separated from Eliza and Cecelia was too much to bear. And they'd certainly be stuck with Head Mistress Tanner since she was now their legal guardian.

"What a mess," Adele whispered as the tears continued to stream down her cheeks. She squeezed her eyes shut and a flickering image of her mother and father laughing on the front porch came to her. The image was blurry but she remembered that day. They had just eaten supper and everyone was out on the front porch. Her father had made some joke and her mother had burst out laughing. Then she'd turned to Adele and smiled warmly at her. Adele remembered the feeling more than the memory. She knew then that her mother loved her and loved her with everything she had. But if she'd loved her, why did she send them all here? Couldn't she have made it work, somehow?

At this, Adele felt the tears began flowing again. She didn't try to stop them. She allowed herself to feel the self-pity. She hated feeling sorry for herself but couldn't stop. She put her head back on her knees and started crying again. Just as she did that, she heard something—a rustle—then a scratch as if something was being pushed towards her. Then she felt something hit the side of her foot.

She jumped a little and stared down at the floor. There was a big, black book at her feet. The creepy feeling she got from the sudden appearance of this strange book was enough to send her out of the closet, out of the basement and back upstairs. But something told her not to be scared. Something told her to stay and to take a look at it.

She looked around, wondering where the book had come from. Had it fallen from the ceiling? She looked up. Nope, there was no way. Then she stared at the book, studying it. It was old, so old that the edges were frayed. The leather was well-worn and the title of the book, once embossed, was all but worn off. She stared at the title, trying to make at least one word out but none of the letters would form to their original shape. And then it was like something started commanding her…

Pick it up. Pick it up. Pick it up.

Adele looked around, wondering if the command was coming from an outside source or from her own mind. She didn't hear anything; it was as if she just felt the words. *Pick it up, pick it up, pick it up…* She also wondered if she'd gone crazy, too, as things like this never happened, not in real life.

Pick it up. Pick it up. Pick it up.

She picked it up. Why not? She had somehow found herself in this situation and now she had to find a way out of it. Or possibly through it. The book was heavy in her hands, which were still stinging with pain. But she wasn't focused on the pain anymore. She was focused on the book. It was thick with pages and pages of something. Adele ran her hand across the title and was able to make out a few letters. There was an "M" as well as a "G" and then there was a "B" too. She paused and kept feeling of the letters. She finally figured out the first word and it was, simply, "Book."

Huh. Book. Well, duh. It was a book.

She went back to feeling the letters, wondering for a second why she didn't just open the thing up or even flip a light on or something, but she couldn't help herself from playing this mystery game. And then the second word came, "Of."

Book Of. Now that was an odd title.

She kept it up, figuring out the "M" and then an "I" and then another "C" and then… It was "Magic."

The Big Book of Magic.

The Big Book of Magic? Magic? Adele shook her head and really started concentrating on the title. She had to figure this out. She kept running her fingers over the letters and finally made out two more words: For Girls. Then she had it—*The Big Book of Magic for Girls.*

The Big Book of Magic for Girls? What was that? She thought about it, then felt some more, trying to figure out the subtitle. And then it came, "*A Beginners Guide to Spells, Curses and the Life of a Witch.*"

The Big Book of Magic for Girls: A Beginners Guide to Spells, Curses and the Life of a Witch.

Magic? Spells? Curses? The hairs on the back of her neck stood up and she felt goosebumps rise on her skin. Adele knew what magic was. She had been taught in church that it was bad, wrong. You weren't supposed to mess with stuff like that. The fear rose up in her swiftly and she knew she'd crossed some line. She had to get out of there. She had to get out of there! And she had to do it now.

She pushed the book away from her and jumped up, running out of the basement like it was on fire. She ran all the way to her bed, climbed in and closed her eyes. She lay there for a long time wondering what, exactly, had just happened and why it had happened to her.

The Big Book of Magic for Girls

The next day, Adele arose with the other girls, got ready for the day and did her chores under the constant, close supervision of Ms. Ingles. She briefly thought about how they were constantly being watched but pushed the thought out of her mind as there wasn't anything she could do about it other than to accept that this was part of being at Bancroft House.

She also pushed everything that had happened the previous night out of her mind and refused think about it, even though the pain in her hands was still almost unbearable. There were two, deep red ugly welts that made it hard for her to hold onto anything. But she didn't dwell on any of it, not on the pain, not on the incidents that had happened. She had decided that she was going to do her time, as Jane as said, and that when she was old enough she would leave Bancroft House, get a job and then send for her sisters. That would be some time in the future but she'd do it. It was her only choice.

When the other girls got to breakfast, Head Mistress Tanner pulled Adele to the side and into the kitchen.

"You will not be allowed to eat in the dining room again," she told her and pointed to a rickety old table and chair in the corner. "You will take your meals right there from now on. Understood?"

Adele nodded and was almost grateful that she was still going to be allowed meals. The thought of them never letting her eat again had crossed her mind several times.

"And no more serving," she said. "You will wash dishes every day instead."

Adele nodded. She was beyond caring.

"I've spoken to the father of the girl you assaulted and he told me to keep you away from her. If anything else happens, you will be expelled."

Adele nodded, thinking that might not be so bad. Then she immediately felt bad when she thought of her sisters who needed her. No, she would do what needed to be done. She would get through this and she would find a way to get out of here and take her sisters with her.

"Don't misbehave again," the head mistress snapped and then turned on her heel and left the room.

Adele watched her go, then sat down at the table and waited on breakfast. It arrived in about five minutes, being served by Lotta, who gave her a weak smile before going into the dining room with her tray. She glanced at it, then smiled. It was a plate of steaming eggs, hash browns and crispy bacon. There was even a piece of fresh toast with butter cut into two little triangles.

Adele glanced around, saw that no one was watching and dove in. It was the best thing she'd eaten since she'd gotten there, except, maybe, the pudding the previous night. Even so, Adele appreciated what Lotta had done for her. She would be sure to thank her later.

Once breakfast had been eaten, and the dishes cleaned, it was down to the conservatory to work on the flowers. There, she avoided Jane's eyes all morning but she knew she'd confront her sooner rather than later. She was at one of the tables removing thorns from some roses with a small pair of pruning shears when Jane walked up to her. Adele ignored her and wished she'd just go away.

When she didn't speak to her, Jane snapped, "Well, aren't you going to say anything, Mountain Girl?"

Adele turned to her and said, "No."

"No what?"

"No, I am not going to say anything and no to the fact that you will never again call me Mountain Girl. If you do, you will regret it, Jane. That stops right here, right now."

Jane gulped and looked away, then back at her. "I don't mean anything by it."

"I don't care," Adele said. "Now leave me alone."

"Well, aren't you going to say anything?"

"About what?" Adele asked.

"You know what," she said and then whispered, "About what happened last night."

Adele stripped off a thorn and refused to look at her. She said, "As far as I am concerned, nothing happened last night, Jane."

Before Jane could answer, she turned to her and held up her hands, palm facing. Jane's eyes widened at the red, ugly welts.

"Oh, my God," Jane muttered.

"That's right," she told her. "I took the fall for you. It was the first time and it will be the last time."

"Well," she said. "Whatever. Well, you... You, uh... You messed it all up for me. Now they're be patrolling the kitchen and I won't get to eat."

"What do I care if you eat?" Adele said, her voice rising. "You are what is called a turn-coat. You'd sell anyone down the river if you thought it'd make you look better and keep the heat off of you."

"Shut up," Jane said. "You just shut up right now!"

"Why?" Adele asked. "We're not friends and we never will be."

Jane's mouth dropped.

"Girls!"

They turned to see Sally staring at them. She raised an eyebrow and Adele turned back to her work, deciding to ignore Jane for the rest of her life.

Jane stared at her, then whispered, "Look, I'm sorry."

Then she walked away. For a moment, Adele felt bad, like she shouldn't have been so harsh. It wasn't Jane's fault things were the way they were, but she knew she could never trust her. Adele sighed and stared at the rose she'd been working on, then glanced at the pile she still had to do. It seemed as high as a mountain. It would take her all day to do that pile but Sally would want it done in half that time. More, more, more. That's what they wanted. It's a wonder they didn't ask for the other girls' souls while they were at it.

She got back to work and as she worked, her mind kept going back to the book. The book, the book, the book. What did it mean? Where had it come from? Could there be some evil force trying to get her to do something bad? Adele was not a bad person. The thought of harming anyone, even someone like Jane, repulsed her.

She continued to turn the situation over and over in her mind as she picked up the pace to get the flowers done. She was so distracted that she cut her thumb with the shears. Blood squirted out of her finger and onto the roses. The blood just dissolved into the petals and disappeared. She watched it happen, wondering if she should throw the roses out or if anyone would notice. There would be big trouble over this, she was sure. She quickly wrapped her finger with her shirt tail and wondered what she was going to do about it.

Sally came up behind her and groaned loudly. "Go to the nurse."

Adele only nodded, not speaking directly to her as she'd been taught, then raced out of the conservatory and up to the main house. She knew exactly where the nurses' office was and was about to go right to it. But something stopped her. It was curiosity. She wanted to see just exactly what was going on in the rich girl's classroom. She took her time to walk past one of the classrooms and peer in at the students who were being taught by a well dressed, well coiffed middle-aged woman.

"Merci," she said, obviously speaking French.

"Merci," the girls replied.

The teacher said something else in French, it was repeated and then all the girls erupted in giggles. The teacher laughed, too, and then shook her head, calling the class to order once again.

Adele stared at the girls, longing to be in there with them, studying, learning, doing something other than what she was doing. The rich girls looked so happy, so contented. This caused jealousy to rise up swiftly in her and she felt it so hard her head almost swam with it. It wasn't fair, none of it was fair. It wasn't fair that her daddy had died or that her mother had given them away to this awful place. It wasn't fair that these pretty rich girls got all the breaks in life and she got none. It wasn't fair that her little sister's hands were covered in scratches and cuts. It wasn't fair that they went to bed hungry every single night. None of it was fair and Adele was good and tired of things not being fair.

There had to be a way. Then she remembered the book. Maybe magic wasn't bad. Maybe magic wasn't evil. Maybe magic was her way out.

Stop it! she told herself. *No. No and absolutely no.*

Magic was wrong, she told herself. She couldn't even allow herself to consider that option. And, besides, she didn't even know if it was real. Was it real? She didn't know. She shook herself and went to the nurses' office, pausing at the door to read the sign: Nurse Clarice Sinclair. Adele stared at the name for a moment before opening the door. The pretty young nurse, outfitted in a white uniform and a small white nurse's cap, stared up at her, startled. Apparently, she'd been engrossed in something she was reading. Adele smiled at her. She'd seen her before, of course. The woman had floated into the dining room a few times since she'd been at Bancroft House but had never said anything to her. She seemed to be well liked by the rich girls, probably because she was younger and prettier than the head mistress or her lackey, Ms. Ingles. She would joke with the rich girls and sometimes sit with them and eat dinner. She made them laugh and smile and she never, not once that Adele knew of, glanced in the other girls' direction. It was as if they, too, were invisible to her.

"Yes?" the nurse said, still looking startled.

"I cut my finger," Adele said and held it up. "My thumb, actually."

The nurse shoved whatever it was she was reading away into her desk then got up and came over to Adele, inspected her finger and shook her head. "That's a bad cut. I've told them to get you girls some gloves but they never listen to me."

Adele nodded.

The nurse started to say something else but stopped and stared at her hands, then turned them around to reveal the welts from the paddling.

"What did you do?" she asked and stared into Adele's eyes.

"Uh, nothing," Adele said, not wanting to share how she got the wounds.

The nurse stared at her, then shook her head. "Well, there's not much I can do for the welts, but I can stitch the thumb."

Adele breathed a sigh of relief. "Thanks, Nurse Sinclair."

"Oh, just call me Nurse Clarice," she said and smiled at her. "That's what all the girls call me."

Adele nodded.

"I'll get you stitched right up," she said gently.

Adele appreciated her kindness and the nurse had her finger cleaned and stitched in no time.

"And who are you?" Nurse Clarice asked as she finished stitching.

"Adele," she said. "Adele Clemmons."

"Oh, yes," the nurse said. "You and your sisters are relatively new here."

"Yes, we are," Adele said.

"You were supposed to be brought in for a checkup," she said.

"Oh?" Adele asked.

She nodded, got up and went over to her desk and started looking around for something. "Wonder why that was overlooked?"

"I'm not sure."

She stopped and studied her for a second. "All new students are supposed to have a checkup upon admission. I've asked but no one's sent you three over. Well, you're here now, so let me do it," she said, picking up a clipboard and a pen.

Adele didn't know how to decline, so she allowed the nurse to check her blood pressure, prick her finger and do all that other checkup stuff, all the while making notations on her clipboard. It only took a few minutes and she was done.

"I'll send your blood to the lab to check for anemia and whatnot," she said, feeling her throat. "But you look fine."

Adele nodded and the nurse smiled at her.

"Tell them to take it easy on you the rest of the day," the nurse said and sat down, tossed the clipboard to the side and wrote something on a notepad. "I mean it. I get one of you girls in here every day of the week with a cut like that. Sometimes I think that's the only reason they employ me."

She tore the paper off and handed it to Adele. Adele took it, glanced over it and saw that she was being excused from work for the rest of the day by the nurse. Not that it would ever fly with Sally but Adele appreciated her concern.

"Thanks," she said and smiled at the nurse.

She returned her smile and said, "You're very welcome."

Adele stared at her, wondering why, if this woman knew these children were in danger, she didn't do something about it. But then, Jane's words came back to her and she understood that most people couldn't do anything about anything. It was always best, and usually easier, to just look the other way. But Nurse Clarice was the nicest person she had met in this whole miserable place. She was so nice, it seemed as though she didn't even belong there. Adele longed to ask her why she would work at such a place but she knew that people had to earn their living some way. Besides, the nurse might not even know what went on. Or, if she did, she might just turn a blind eye. Also, she might tell the headmistress what she had said.

Adele decided not to worry about it. She thanked the nurse for stitching her finger up and was about to leave when she halted her.

"Oh, wait," she said and reached into a big jar filled with suckers. "Here's a lollipop."

Adele almost laughed. She was much too old for a lollipop but she knew that Cecelia would love it. "Thanks," she said and took it. "I appreciate it."

"You're very welcome," she said. "Oh, wait, you forgot this."

Adele wondered what she was talking about. Forgot what? She watched as the nurse went to her desk, rummaged around and picked up a big, black book. She started over towards Adele with it. Adele's eyes grew wide when she saw that it was, in fact, the very book she'd found in the basement. She stared at the book, then at the nurse, wondering what was going on and how she could get out of this.

"It's heavy," Nurse Clarice said with a smile and held it out for Adele.

"It's not mine," she said, shaking it off. There was no way she was going to touch that book.

"But it is, isn't it?" she said, smiling at her. "It's your book. Your name is in the front of it."

She opened it up and showed Adele the inscription: "Property of Adele Clemmons."

Adele was dumfounded but what could she do? She had to take the thing now, didn't she? But why did the nurse have it? Maybe Adele had lost her mind. Maybe nothing in this place was real, not the nurse or the flower factory or even herself. Her mind spun with the anxiety of not knowing what exactly was going on. She had to find something to hold onto, something to bring her back to reality. She thought about her sisters and found comfort in that.

"Adele?" the nurse said.

Adele opened her eyes and stared at her. "It's not my book."

The nurse looked at her like she didn't believe her. "Well, just take it anyway," she replied. "You can take it back to the stables."

"The stables?"

"Yes," she said. "If you don't know what to do with it, take it to the stables. When this house was built, they built stables for the horses. Now they're used as some sort of study room. Take it there and see what you can do with it. It does have your name on it."

Maybe the nurse was the one who'd lost her mind. Even so, Adele knew she wasn't about to let her leave the room without taking the book. So she took it. The nurse smiled at her, told her to take it easy the rest of the day, then went to her desk and sat down. Adele backed out of the room holding the book tight and then hurried down the hall and out of the house and towards the stables.

As the nurse had indicated, the stables had been converted into study rooms, obviously for the rich girls. There were several big leather Chesterfield couches and a few big oak tables with nice chairs scattered around them. There was even a big TV in the back, which wasn't turned on. The space was nice, airy and open and very conducive to studying.

The study room was empty when Adele entered. She looked around and found a big, comfy looking leather chair facing the window. She walked over, sat down and took a deep breath. This was it. This was something. She didn't know what it was, but it was something.

Now what? She tentatively opened the book and began to flip through it, trying to make some sense of it. However, the book was even more confusing than the French the rich girls had been speaking in class. Adele couldn't make heads or tails out of it because parts were written in some language she couldn't understand.

She continued to study the book and then something began to happen. Suddenly, it started to make sense to her. She began to realize that the book was made up of different spells, lots and lots of spells that, if used properly, could change the course of things. Within the spells she could make things happen that would have never even occurred to her to do before. Also, the sentences began to form ideas and the ideas planted themselves into her head and the ideas in her head came to have meaning, practical meaning. Even the parts written in the foreign language began to make sense, which perplexed as well as excited her. She wondered how she was able to understand it, but then realized it just didn't matter. *Yes*, she thought, *I can do this*.

She didn't know what took her over, but all of a sudden she stood up, turned around and said, "*Open*."

Nothing happened.

Adele shook her head. What was she trying to do? What had the book said? She couldn't remember but the basic premise was this: Start small, practice, get better, move onto bigger things.

Start small, practice, get better, move onto bigger things.

Adele took a deep breath and tried again. "Open," just then realizing she was trying to open the door at the far end of the room. It wasn't happening, though. She shook herself, wondered for a split second what she was doing, then shouted, "*Open!*"

Nothing.

"*Open up!*" she shouted then took a breath. Why was she doing this? Why was she trying to open a door with the sheer will of her mind? She glanced at the book, then ran her hand down the page. As she did this, it seemed as though she felt something move through her, so much so she jumped back. Wow. Oh, wow. It felt like electricity, but then she realized that it was magic, which put her doubts about it being real to rest. Oh, yes, it was real, *very* real. There was actual magic in the book and it was beginning to take form inside of Adele. She breathed heavily and turned back to the door. She could do this; she knew she could do this.

"*Open!*" she shouted at the door.

Nothing, nothing, nothing.

"Good grief!" Adele exclaimed and fell down in the chair, covering her eyes with her hands. Why did nothing work out for her? Why was she always in a state of frustrated angst? Life wasn't fair; it just wasn't fair, not to her, not to her sisters. She was tired, so tired of her life being like this. When she thought of the days and weeks and months that it would take for her to be able to leave this miserable place, she wanted to burst into tears.

No. She was not giving up. She would not give up. She had to have something in her life, anything to take her mind off the misery. So, without thought, the frustration got the best of her and she jumped up, pointed at the door and yelled, "*Open!*"

The door flew open with such force Adele's hair blew from the draft. Adele's mouth dropped and she was so shocked that she'd been able to do that, to force a door to open just by using her will, she got scared. She almost ran out of the room and away from Bancroft House.

What now? She didn't know. She didn't know what this meant or where to go from here. She didn't even really know how she got here or why. It started with the book… No it started with the girl in the dining room… No, it started with…

She squeezed her eyes shut and a vision came to her. She was back home with her family. Her father was still alive, her mother still happy. Her sisters were well fed and beautiful and she was there, too, feeling the love she'd always felt at home. Tears streamed down her cheeks and she felt that love swell up inside of her so much she thought she'd burst from it. The vision felt so real that she began to question where it was coming from and whether or not it was authentic. Was it coming from her or from the book?

She opened her eyes and stared at the book. The vision was coming from the book, almost as if it were trying to comfort her or something. Before she could consider that, she had another vision. This one was real. A man speaking to her mother. Chills went up and down her spine as the vision came to her. And then she knew. She knew what had happened. How she knew she didn't know. But it was Mr. Adams. He was there at her house speaking to her mother. Her mother nodded and then smiled.

"Boarding school?" she said. "Why, we'd never be able to afford that. Besides, I love having my girls with me."

And then she saw him slipping her a card and turning his head towards the flower garden. Adele watched him from the side, wondering what he was up to. And then he turned to Adele and started to speak.

"Don't tell me," Adele said to herself.

"We wanted you because you know so much about flowers," he said. "That's why you were brought here. To work. Now get back to work."

Adele's eyes popped open. Head Mistress Tanner was staring at the door, staring at her.

"What are *you* doing in here?" she snapped. "You're supposed to be working."

Adele, shaken from the vision and what it meant, couldn't answer her. It was like it was fate or something that she and her sisters were brought here. She shook her head then stared down at the floor where the book lay, still open to the passage she'd been reading. She kicked it under the chair and straightened up.

"The nurse told me to come in here," she said. "She told me to take the day off, to rest."

"I don't care what she said," she told her. "You are not allowed in here and you know that. Now get back to work."

Adele nodded, not wanting to butt heads with the head mistress. There were other important things to think about, to take care of, least of all what she was going to do with what had just happened. And what had happened? What was this? Was it a step in the right direction? Was it clarification about what had happened to bring her and her sisters here? Or was it, simply, a new way of thinking about things? Was it a way out of Bancroft House? She didn't know but she did know that she wanted to hang onto the feeling this little bit of magic gave her.

Come Now

Of course, Adele didn't tell anyone about the book or what had happened. She knew to keep quiet. But for the rest of the day, whenever she'd think about it, she'd get goosebumps. What was going on? And why was this happening to her?

That night at dinner, she sat in her sad little corner and picked over her dull meal of one hamburger patty, a lump of mashed potatoes and a stale roll. She thought about the food she'd eaten that morning and looked over at the cooks, all three of them. They were all big, burly women with plain faces and dressed in white restaurant-type uniforms. They ignored her and tended to their work. As she watched them, she wondered how they could feed the other girls the meals they did. She figured it was just part of their jobs and they probably didn't worry about it too much. But how she longed to get up and go over there and grab a bite of the good food that they sent out to the rich girls.

Then she thought about the book and she felt shivers go up her spine. What was she going to do about that? And how was she going to get it back? She knew it was safe under the chair in the study room, but for how long was anyone's guess. She had to find a way to get it back. She couldn't leave it there forever. She didn't want anyone to find it.

Her thought were interrupted by Ms. Clarice, the nurse. She floated into the kitchen through the swinging door and looked around. Then she smiled when she saw Adele.

"Oh, there you are," she said, walking over. "I wanted to check on your thumb."

"Oh, it's fine," Adele said and held it up.

"Did you have to go back to work?" she asked, giving her a sympathetic look.

"I did," Adele replied. "But it's okay."

She nodded, looking around. "Why are you in here?"

"I'm not allowed to eat in there anymore," Adele said, then immediately kicked herself for sounding so self-pitying.

"Oh," she said, not involving herself. "That's too bad. Anyway, that's all I wanted. Have a nice meal."

She gave Adele a pleasant smile and turned to walk away. Adele immediately wanted to ask her something and stood.

"Nurse Clarice?" she called.

"Yes?" she said, turning back around.

"What about the book?"

She stared at her for a moment, blinking her eyes as if she didn't quite understand. "Uh, I don't have anything to do with the books, dear. I'm just the nurse."

"No," Adele said. "Not the text books. The book you gave me today."

"Excuse me?"

"I just wanted to know…" Adele started, then stopped. She took a breath and continued, "Why did you give me that book?"

"What book?" she asked. "You came in because of your injury and then I gave you a checkup, that's all."

Adele stared at her. Why wasn't she admitting that she'd given her the book? What was the big deal? She only wanted to know where it came from and from whom. That's all.

"But you gave it to me," Adele said. "It was big, black book? Don't you remember?"

The nurse was getting perturbed. She crossed her arms and said, "I don't know what you're implying, but I don't appreciate the insinuation."

Adele studied her. She really didn't know what she was talking about. She had no idea that she'd even given her the book. She was telling the truth. *What was going on?*

Just then, a cook walked by on her way to the sink with a huge aluminum stockpot. As she passed them, she said, "She doesn't even know she did it," the cook said. "Leave her alone. You're scaring the absolute tar out of her."

"What did you say?" Adele asked her.

The cook set the pot on the counter and turned to her. "Just shut up about it or she'll report you."

Adele stared back at the nurse. She blinked at her. It was as if she hadn't heard what the cook was saying to her. In fact, she hadn't.

Adele's mind began to swirl. This was too weird, too creepy. *What was going on?*

The cook shrugged and turned to clean the pot. Adele stared at her, then back at Nurse Clarice who shook her head and walked over to her and stared into her eyes. Adele stared back and wondered what was going on. Then she knew. Then she got it. None of them knew what was going on; it was like they were being taken over and the book was sending her messages through them. But what if it wasn't the book? What if it was something else? Adele didn't know. All she knew was that *something* was making these people do these things that they weren't even aware that they were doing. Knowing that sent shivers of fear up and down her spine. It was suddenly too much and Adele felt sick, like she wanted to throw up and pass out at the same time. She also knew to cover her tracks, so she said, "I'm sorry. I'm just so weak. They don't give us much food."

"You poor dear," Nurse Clarice said and smoothed the hair back from her face. "Here, let me give you something."

She pulled out something from her jacket pocket and held it out to Adele. It was a chocolate bar with nuts, Adele's favorite. It was also the same candy bar she'd seen in Head Mistress Tanner's desk. Had the nurse taken it or did the head mistress give it to her? Adele didn't know and she certainly didn't want to take the candy bar now. There was something really strange going on here.

"Take it," she said.

Adele nodded, took the candy bar and watched as the nurse exited the room.

"Oh, by the way, you need to send your sisters in for their checkup," she called at the door. "Don't forget, Adele."

Adele nodded. "Okay. Bye."

"Bye."

Adele watched her go, turned back to her meal, then stared at the candy bar. Without thinking, she unwrapped it and took a big bite, sighing with pleasure at its sweet, chocolate taste. It had been too long since she'd eaten something so sweet and delicious. As she ate, she thought about the situation and became afraid and the fear made her decide that she would not go after the book. She decided that the book was trouble and she had had enough of that. Besides, who knew what might happen if she actually used some of those spells in that book? She didn't even understand them and realized she might not ever. In the wrong hands, the book would be bad and she decided she wasn't ready for anything like that. She might do something terrible, like open the gates of hell or something! She almost laughed at the thought but the odd behavior of the staff was too much to bear and she had a strange suspicion that the book was behind it and that she'd somehow caused it. She just didn't know how.

She sighed again with pleasure at the candy bar and felt certain of her decision. She would just do her time at Bancroft House and then get out and start a whole new life. That's what she would do. Just a few years and she'd be done then she and her sisters could leave for good. Why, her fifteenth birthday was coming up in December and then it would be only three years until she was of age and could take care of her siblings.

She smiled. Yeah, only three years. Wow. Then her smile disappeared. That was a long time. Maybe... No. No, forget it. It was too much of a risk.

Adele was so caught up in her thoughts that she didn't notice the cook until she slammed something heavy down on the old table. The fork on her plate rattled as it hit the table.

"Don't leave your junk laying around the kitchen," she snapped. "We don't have room for this nonsense."

Adele looked up at her in horror then saw what she'd thrown on the table. It was *The Big Book of Magic for Girls*. The sinking feeling Adele felt was almost enough to make her run away from Bancroft House once and for all.

But then... The thought came back to her. What if the book could help her get out of here? What if she could learn magic and be able to leave with her sisters? The thought was almost too enticing. She felt excited, but then shook her head. No. She just couldn't.

She stared at the book. But what if she could?

It took her three days to finally open the book again. Three days. After she had gotten over the shock of the cook slamming the book down, she knew she had to hide it. She waited until the cooks got busy, then excused herself to the restroom, then ran all the way to her room, concealing the book under her shirt, though it was hard as it was so large.

There, she stashed it under her bed and prayed no one would find it and for God to forgive her if she was doing evil.

And for three days she tried to pretend that she didn't know anything about the book. The nurse took Cecelia and Eliza out of class for their physicals, then called her in and told her that while Eliza was fine, Cecelia was not. In fact, she was bordering on being anemic.

"She's very weak," she said and handed her a bottle of pills. "Have her take one of these a day. They're iron pills. They'll help her."

Adele took the pills and asked, "What happens when the pills run out?"

Nurse Clarice shrugged. "They should do for a while, but when they run out, I can't help you. I don't have the budget for it. You will have to figure something out yourself, Adele."

Figure something out? What could she do? She didn't have any money for iron supplements or any way to get any. But she knew she'd have to find a way. Cecelia had been acting very strangely since she'd been at Bancroft House. She rarely fussed but she wanted to sleep a lot and was very lethargic. She was also constantly complaining about being cold and the shabby gray cardigan sweater she wore, identical to the ones all the other girls wore, was not much comfort. She could barely hold her head up and do her work. Still the child pushed onward and did what she could. Adele went along behind her and straightened the beds she made, made sure the dishes were clean and the sheets and clothes folded properly so she wouldn't get in trouble. She also kept at close eye on her at the flower factory. But sometimes she just couldn't be there and Cecelia would get yelled at by Ms. Ingles or Sally for doing something wrong. Adele knew it was from malnutrition. The child needed better food. She needed vitamins.

That's why Adele finally broke down and realized that magic might be the only way that Cecelia could get better. She was the only person that could help Cecelia and she would do whatever she had to do in order to save her.

So, on the third day after the reappearance of the book at dinner, Adele screwed up her courage and retrieved it from beneath her bed after all the other girls had gone to sleep. It was, obviously, too dark to read it in the room, so she'd have to go downstairs somewhere and find an inconspicuous corner.

Adele crept out of bed, holding the book tightly to her chest and left the room. She walked through the house until she was on the first floor, then she turned and looked around. The library was just off the dining room and there were several table lamps. She went in, glancing around the enormous room filled with floor to ceiling bookshelves which were overstuffed with all kinds of books. Part of her longed to grab a few and look at them, but she didn't have time.

She finally found a small desk in the corner that had a lamp on it in the form of a white fish. She sat down in the small leather chair, put the book on the desk, turned on the light and opened it, not caring to which page. Oddly enough, it opened on a description of what exactly a witch was.

She read the description, noticing that there wasn't anything evil or bad about it, which set her at ease. She read about what it entailed, doing good and using white magic to help others. She liked that idea, especially if she could help herself and her sisters. Then she skimmed the page and read about something called black magic, which was the opposite of white magic. It was about casting spells on people who you feel have done wrong to you or those you love. *Well, that list would certainly be long*, she thought to herself and chuckled. She read on and found that the descriptions were pretty fundamental. Adele realized that she understood the basic premise of it.

She took a breath and read on, then turned the page, which described how magic worked. She found out that you did it all with your mind, connecting with the powers of the world to bring about the desired result. That sounded interesting. She thought she could do that, maybe.

She kept flipping through the book and then came to a section describing how to physically make objects move, like the door the other day. She read it with interest, really concentrating on the words and allowing then to sink into her head. She thought she'd give that a try again and see if it were any easier.

She stood from the chair, looked around the library and noticed an interesting looking book to her left. The spine read, *Insects and Their World*. She smiled to herself, thinking of Eliza, who loved insects. She wanted that book.

Now to do it.

She held up her hand, really concentrated on the book and said, "*Come.*"

The book didn't move.

She took a breath and said, "*Come,*" again.

Nothing.

Another breath, more concentration and then, "*Come now.*"

Nope.

She was about to give up went she remembered a passage in the book, "*If you want to make things happen, you have to use the force within you to make it happen. There is a stillness, a quiet place from which magic comes. Tap into that and bring forth your desired result. However, you mustn't try too hard. Trying too hard will only result in frustration. It is a little like trying to make sense of a Rorschach test. No amount of forcing will bring an image to your mind. Just allow the image to come to you and be whatever it is that you envision it to be."*

A Rorschach test? Oh! The inkblot test thing. Adele understood what the book was telling her immediately. You just had to let it happen. And then... A stillness, a quiet place. Adele closed her eyes and thought of her quiet place, deep down inside of her, the place where her courage and her ability resided. It was there that she found the connection she needed to move forward with this. There, in that place deep inside of her, was a great strength just waiting to be utilized. And so she did.

"*Come,*" she told the book. The book, still stubborn but giving in a little, rattled in the shelf.

Adele tapped into the quiet place again and said with more vindication, "*Come.*"

The book flew off the shelf and fell to the floor. That was something. She was getting closer. But she now had to get it up off the floor and into the air and somehow into her possession. She was beginning to understand that you just couldn't take something; you had to command it to be yours. That's what she was trying to do.

"*Come!*" she said. The book rose about a foot off the floor, then fell back down, opening in half. She stared at it and wondered what to do next. She was trying her best but it still wasn't budging.

She started to try again when, all of a sudden, someone said, "Ugh, you're doing it wrong!"

Adele jerked and looked around wildly. Who was there? Was it Head Mistress Tanner? If so, she would be in some major trouble and she just didn't want to any more trouble. Was it Jane? Had she followed her down her to get back in her good graces, which she ought to know Adele would never allow? Once you crossed her, she crossed you off the list.

She was surprised. It was neither of them. It was someone completely different, someone new. Out of the dark recesses of the room, the young girl came across the room to her. Who was she? Adele had never seen her before, but figured she had to be one of the rich girls. Maybe she'd just arrived or maybe she'd been on some break. She didn't know. Sometimes that happened. Sometimes one of the rich girls would leave for a few weeks and then come back. Sometimes not. Or sometimes there was a new one that would show up. No one ever told the other girls anything about them so she knew very little about their world. Besides, there were so many of them that Adele had trouble keeping up, especially now that she'd been sequestered in the kitchen during meals. But this girl was definitely new. But then again, she might have been a new other girl, though her clothes looked almost new and her hair was styled to perfection. Adele didn't know what to think about her and really wanted to know what she wanted. And if she planned on ratting her out to Head Mistress Tanner.

The girl smiled slightly at Adele and stopped in front of her, leaning against the bookshelf with her hands behind her back. Adele suddenly felt intimidated. She was definitely one of the rich girls, as she was dressed just like them. She was a beautiful girl with long, thick blonde hair and gorgeous blue eyes. Her skin was like porcelain. It was so white, it looked almost iridescent.

She didn't say anything and just stood looking at Adele as if she expected Adele to start the conversation. When Adele kept quiet, she sighed loudly and said, "What are you *trying* to do?"

Adele shrugged, not wanting to disclose any information on her activities.

"Well, it's not working, is it?"

"What do you mean?" Adele asked and narrowed her eyes at her.

"I can't stand it anymore," she said and held her hand. "Give it to me."

"What?"

"The book," she said. "*The Big Book of Magic for Girls*."

"How do you know about that?"

She smiled. "Who cares how I know? Just give it to me."

Even though Adele thought better of it, she retrieved the book and took it to her. As she held it out to her, the girl merely rolled her eyes and said, "Go back to where you were in the book."

Adele studied her but for some reason did as she was instructed, opening the book to the chapter she'd been reading. She then held it out to the girl, who merely skimmed it, then looked at her.

"Did you even read this?" she asked.

"Of course I did."

"No, not carefully, you didn't," she said. "You're doing it all wrong. You're trying to force things and you never force magic."

"I'm not trying to do magic."

"Listen, I know," she said and scoffed. "It's not a big deal to me. Just stop trying so hard. If you had read more carefully, you have realized that forcing anything is a surefire way to never get it done."

"Then what am I supposed to do?"

"Relax," she said. "It's supposed to be fun."

It was? Adele hadn't thought of it like that.

"Now try again," the girl said.

Adele glanced at her, wondering if she should even be doing this in front of her. What if the girl was tricking her to try to make her look foolish? She pushed the thought from her mind, stepped back, focused on the insect book and said, "*Come to me.*"

The book didn't budge. It continued to lay there flat and arrogant. It was as if the book had taken on a personality, one that wasn't very accommodating. That's when Adele knew that it had. That book symbolized her small step from the real world and into the world of magic. If she could conquer that book, she'd be on her way. But was that what she wanted? Did she want that? She didn't know but she did know she needed something else in her life besides the chores and hardships of Bancroft House.

"Put the book down," the girl told her. "You have to free yourself to receiving the book."

Adele nodded, put the book down and concentrated back on the insect book.

"You can do it," the girl whispered quietly. "Just tell it what you want. Tell it to come to you. That's all you have to do. Not force, just suggestion. It *will* come to you."

Adele nodded.

"Clear you mind," she whispered softly. "Clear you mind and ask for what you desire."

Adele did just that, pushing everything but the thought of the book out of her mind. She owned the book. It was her book. It was her time. Without a thought, she raised her hand and said, "*Come now.*"

The book rose swiftly but gently, flew through the air and dropped into Adele's hands. It fell open to an oversized picture of a praying mantis. A big grin broke out across Adele's face and she stared at the girl with joy only accomplishment can bring.

"See? It's easy," the girl said and tapped her head. "It's all in here, everything. If you are fixated on failing, instead of succeeding, you will concrete on the failure instead of the win, so much so until the failure becomes your reality."

"What does that mean?"

"Expect to fail and you will," she said.

"I don't expect to fail," Adele said and put the book back on the shelf.

The girl laughed. "Oh, really? If I hadn't come in here, you would have been here all night and tomorrow too, wondering why you couldn't do it. And the reason why is because you expect to fail at it. You were begging that book to come to you instead to telling it to. Which means that you never really expected it to come to you in the first place."

Adele thought about that. She was right.

The girl continued, "Take failure out of the equation and allow your mind to open wide with possibilities and you will discover that things will go your way. Without force. Remember that. No forcing. No begging."

Adele took all that in, making a note to enforce it in her life, then said, "Who are you?"

"Who are you?" she asked back and smiled secretively.

"Adele."

She nodded. "I know. Adele Clemmons."

"How do you know my name?"

"I've seen you around," she said and shrugged.

"I haven't seen you around," Adele said. "Did you just get here?"

"No, I've been here a while."

"And who are you?" Adele asked, almost getting frustrated.

"I'm Jolene."

Adele nodded and started to hold out her hand for her to shake then thought better of it. That was a little too formal and she could tell this girl might not like it. For some reason, Adele wanted to like her, and for her to return the favor. She hadn't had a real friend since she'd gotten to Bancroft House and the thought of being able to just talk to someone else was almost exhilarating. For some reason, she felt as if this girl would understand her and she really needed understanding.

Just then, a clock somewhere in the library chimed. Adele turned to it and saw that it was almost after two.

"It's late," Jolene said. "You better get back to bed."

"You too," Adele said.

She nodded. "It's okay. I don't sleep much. But you go. I'll see you around."

Adele nodded and started out of the room. She stopped, turned around and said, "Thanks for helping me."

"It's been my pleasure," she replied and smiled at her. "Remember, no forcing, Adele."

Adele nodded, gave a little wave and started to make her way back to bed.

"Wait," she said. "You forgot your book."

She nodded at *The Big Book of Magic for Girls*, which was still on the floor where Adele had placed it.

"Oh," Adele said and went back and retrieved the book and tucked it under her arm. "Thanks."

"No, thank you," she said. "See you later."

The next morning, Adele made her way into the dining room with the other girls. She looked around for Jolene and spotted her sitting with the other rich girls in the middle of the long table. Adele smiled at her and gave a little wave. Jolene returned the wave with a friendly smile.

"Who are you waving to?" Eliza asked.

"No one," Adele said, feeling oddly defensive.

Lotta, who was walking with them, looked at Adele, then towards Jolene. A peculiar look crossed her face but she didn't say anything. Adele knew she wouldn't approve of her being friends with a rich girl and she really wasn't up for a lecture on it. Besides, Adele liked the idea of being friends with Jolene. She could tell she was going to be one of the popular girls and that's because she was, at heart, a nice person. This made Adele feel cool by association and that really wasn't a bad feeling to have. It actually gave her something to look forward to.

"Whatever," Eliza said and broke off, going to the other girls' table.

Adele shrugged and then walked towards the swinging door of the kitchen. She was about to go in when she turned around and tried to find Jolene again. But she was gone and another rich girl was sitting down in the seat she had just been in. Where did she go? Probably to the restroom or maybe she forgot a book or something. Regardless, Adele smiled to herself, quite happy that she might have a secret friend, and went into the kitchen for breakfast.

The day dragged on. After breakfast, it was dishes and cleaning the dining room, then work in the house, then to the conservatory and then their classes. Adele sat idly in the room and listened to the teacher, thinking of how she was missing out on any real form of education. All their lessons consisted of stuff she'd already learned in school before she had come to Bancroft House. It was like a refresher course that she didn't need. As a result, the lessons did her no good and she was bored for the two hours they were forced to sit in that room. She sighed, then raised her hand.

"Yes?" Professor Wheaton asked.

"May I be excused?"

"For what reason?"

"Restroom," Adele said.

She shrugged and nodded. Adele stood and left the room, well aware of all the other girls' eyes on her. She didn't have to use the restroom, she just wanted out of that room. During this time, she knew the rich girls were in the billiards room taking a break from their studies.

Adele slipped by the room, barely pausing at the door to see if Jolene might be in there. The room was huge and full of different games. There was a pool table, a dart board and other manly games. She wondered why they had left it like that, but realized some girls might like these types of games. And it would be a shame to get rid of such an elaborate pool table. It was huge and ornately carved and matched the house perfectly.

The room was about half-full of some rich girls who were shooting pool, laughing, talking and, generally, acting like teenagers.

"Gotcha!"

Adele jumped and turned, then saw Jolene behind her laughing.

"You're jumpy," she said, smiling. "What are you doing out?"

"Restroom," Adele said.

Jolene nodded and stared past her into the billiards room. "I don't really like playing boy games."

Adele nodded.

"Want to go outside?" Jolene asked.

"I can't," Adele said. "I have to get back."

"For what?" Jolene asked. "Another lesson on multiples? History that you'll only forget?"

"I like school," Adele said defensively.

"Yeah, well you better go somewhere else, then," Jolene said. "Come on, let's go outside."

Adele knew she shouldn't but she did want a break. Getting out of the house sounded like a good idea, so she followed Jolene out of the door and into a little alcove. They were about to walk across the flagstone patio and into the yard when Adele noticed that there were several rich girls on the patio, enjoying the oddly warm late fall day. Some had their jackets off and others were sipping soda in bottles with straws. With the combination of the backdrop of the bright fall leaves, the preppy look the girls had, and the stone terrace, the entire group looked like an ad for the soda they were drinking. For a moment, Adele longed to be part of their group, then shoved the feeling out of her mind as soon as she saw the girl who had tripped her. She felt like fleeing. She knew the rich girl would tattle on her given the chance.

"I better go back in," Adele whispered to Jolene.

"Why?" Jolene asked and turned to stare at the girls.

"Let's just say, I'm not very well liked by the rich girls."

"Is that what we're called?" Jolene asked and almost burst out laughing.

"Let's go," Adele said. "I don't want to get in trouble."

Just then, a few of the rich girls turned to stare in their direction. Adele glanced to her left and saw another pack coming up the back lawn and towards the house. It was like she was being trapped. The only way out without being seen was through the door. She watched the girls come closer and closer. It was only a matter of time before they saw her and then what was going to happen would happen. Adele didn't want any more trouble.

"Come on," Adele said. "Before they see us."

"I don't have to worry about that," Jolene said and gave her a mischievous grin.

Adele stared at her, wondering what she meant, then glanced at the girls. When she turned back to Jolene, she had disappeared. Adele couldn't believe her eyes. It was like she had disappeared into thin air. It was like she was *there* and then she was *gone*. Adele's heart almost leaped out of her chest. And then she froze. What to do? What to do? She almost panicked but somehow managed to get back though the door and into the house before anyone saw her. She ran all the way to the bathroom where she sat down in an empty stall and tried to get her heart to stop beating so wildly.

"Adele?" a voice called.

It was Professor Wheaton. She sat up straight. "Yes?"

"Are you alright?" she asked. "You've been gone a little too long."

"I'll be okay in a minute," Adele said. "Then I'll be back in."

"Okay," she said and Adele heard the door close.

She breathed a sigh of relief then slumped. What was going on? *What was going on*?!

Adele kept to herself for the rest of the day. She was feeling weird, like someone had played a joke of some sort on her but she couldn't figure out the punch line. Cecelia and Eliza both noticed her odd behavior but didn't comment on it. They were used to her emotional ups and downs and knew to leave her alone. She tried to shake off the eerie feeling she had but it kept coming back. What was going on? She just couldn't figure it out. It was like Jolene was... It was like she wasn't real. And if she wasn't real, that meant Adele was going crazy. And who wouldn't be in this house? What normal young girl wouldn't go nuts living like she lived? It was too much for her.

That was it. She was going crazy. How would she ever be able to hide that? They'd probably lock her away somewhere if they thought she was speaking to people who weren't there! She wanted to burst into tears at the thought and then remembered her poor mother, who might be sick herself. If only she could talk to her, if only she could tell her what was going on, she might be able to make her feel better. But she knew to keep this to herself. She couldn't stand the thought of anyone thinking she was crazy.

Adele didn't know what to do. She only knew that she had to get past this and move on. She decided to just put all of it out of her mind and pretend it didn't exist. Her thoughts were racing with "what if" scenarios and she knew that would get her nowhere. The only thing to do was try to erase the situation from her mind. That was hard, but she really had no choice.

By the time she got into bed that night she was mentally exhausted. She thought she'd have trouble falling asleep but her eyelids got heavy and she found sleep in almost no time. She slept comfortably for a while, then was roused out of sleep by a soft voice which sounded somewhat like her mothers.

"Wake up," the voice called. "Adele...wake up..."

For a minute, she thought she was dreaming, then realized that someone was indeed calling her. She jerked away and almost screamed. Jolene was sitting at the foot of her bed staring at her. Adele's heart began to beat rapidly and the thought of being insane came back to haunt her. *What was going on*?! She didn't know if she could take much more of this.

"You really were asleep," Jolene said. "I've been trying to get you to wake up for almost five minutes."

"What are doing here?" Adele managed to ask.

"Just chilling," she replied and smiled.

Adele looked around the room at all the other girls.

"They're all asleep, especially Big Red over there," she said, jerking her head towards Jane. "Does she snore like that every night?"

Adele glanced at Jane, then back at Jolene. "Yeah, she does."

"Good thing you're a heavy sleeper," she said. "*That* would get annoying."

Adele studied her, whatever she was. Was she an actual human being or a figment of her imagination or just, perhaps, a shadow that looked like a young woman? She knew she had to cast her out of her mind and never look back. She squeezed her eyes shut and tried to eliminate her image.

"What the heck are you doing?" Jolene asked.

"You're not real," Adele said and began to chant. "*You're not real, you're not real, you're not real.*"

Jolene reached over and pinched her.

"Ow!" Adele said and held her arm. "Why did you do that?"

"I didn't," she smarted. "If I'm not real, I didn't do anything. What is wrong with you?"

"You're not real," Adele said. "Now I just have to figure out how to get you out of my mind."

Jolene crossed her arms and leaned back, studying her. "But I am real, Adele."

"You can't be," she said, shaking her head.

"Why can't I be?"

"You just disappeared today!" Adele half-shouted. "If you were real and not a figment of my imagination, you wouldn't have been able to do that."

"I see your point," Jolene said and sighed. "But, I am real. What can I do to prove it to you?"

"You need to go away," Adele told her. "Seriously. You need to leave and never come back."

"Why?"

"Because you're not real!" she said, getting frustrated. "Listen, I don't how I conjured you up or whatever. I guess I have been very lonely, but I need to get my mind straight."

"Excuse me? Conjured *me* up? Please. You don't have that kind of power. In fact, I don't know anyone who does."

"What does that mean?" Adele asked. "I mean... I think... I don't know what's going on. Just leave, okay? Leave and I will forget this happened."

"Whatever," Jolene said. "This is utter nonsense, but whatever. However, I do understand. You've been through a lot. I get it."

"You get what?" Adele asked and then kicked herself for speaking to her. She wasn't real. If someone saw her, they'd think she was talking to herself and then answering, which was the true indicator of being crazy.

"I get it," Jolene said. "You're angry, young, upset. You have a lot of angst, like most teenage girls."

"This isn't angst," Adele scoffed.

"It is," she replied. "I understand, Adele. But I'm here, really here, and you'll just have to get used to that."

"But what are you?"

"What do you mean?"

"Are you real?" she asked. "I mean, I know you're not real, but what are you to me? I mean, am I crazy now?"

Jolene stared at her and then burst out laughing. "What did you think?" she asked, laughing. "That you are hallucinating or something?"

"Yeah, something like that," Adel said, not laughing herself.

"First, if that were true, that would mean you're crazy and you would have conjured me up or something," she said smartly. "Second, if you conjured me up or whatever, I'd be a hallucination. And I'm not. I'm a ghost."

"You're kidding?" Adele said. Of course she was a ghost! Why would a real person want to be friends with her? The thought made her angry and she simmered over it for a few moments until she paused for a second and the words really sank in. This girl was a ghost? A real ghost? How was that possible? And if she was a ghost, how did she get to *be* a ghost? The thought really made Adele nervous so she immediately pushed it out of her mind. She just couldn't think of these things. She just couldn't. It was too real, too much, but at the same time, it was so highly unlikely.

"Please," Jolene said and rolled her eyes. "I'm just a ghost. Big deal."

"How can I be sure?" Adele asked. "How can I be sure you're not a figment of my imagination?"

Jolene considered. "Well, you can't. Not really."

"Then go away and leave me alone."

"I'm not going to do that."

"Why not?"Adele asked. "I didn't invite you into my life."

Jolene laughed again. "I'm a ghost. You don't have to invite a ghost in. We're not vampires."

Adele crossed her arms in a huff and refused to answer her.

"Come on," Jolene said. "Talk to me."

Adele ignored her.

"Please," she said. "What can I do to make you feel better?"

"Just tell me what you want with me," Adele said. "I mean, who are you?"

"I'm Jolene," she said. "I already told you that."

"So what do you want? Do you just want to be friends or something?"

"Uh, no, not exactly," Jolene said. "Listen, we can be friends, sure, but I'm not here to be your friend."

"Then what are you here for?"

"To be your guide."

"My guide?" Adele asked. "What's that?"

She shrugged. "We'll get to that later. But now you need to accept that I am here and that I am real."

"But that might mean I'm crazy."

"Well, if that's what it takes for you to accept me, then that's what it takes."

Adele studied her, then glanced around the room, her eyes settling on Cecelia. She worried about her so much, much more than Eliza. Cecelia was still weak, even with the supplements she'd been getting from the nurse; she needed more food and vitamins. She wished she could do something for her, to make her life better. She'd promised her mother she'd take care of her and every day the girl seemed to withdraw into herself more and more. The thought of it almost made Adele cry and now she had a ghost to deal with which made her feel crazy and even more out of control.

"Listen, Adele," Jolene said. "I'm not here to harm you, or even your sisters."

"Then what are you here for?"

"I told you," she said. "To be your guide."

Adele turned to face her then it hit her. "Magic, right? That's why you're here."

Jolene nodded. "More or less."

"You shoved the book at me, didn't you?" she asked. "In the basement, I mean."

"I did," she said. "And then you kept losing the thing, so I had to keep finding ways to get it back in your hands."

"Did you do something to Nurse Clarice and the cooks?"

Jolene laughed loudly. "That was a hoot! You should have seen your face." She framed her hands around Adele's face like a photographer would and smiled. "Priceless!"

"Or scary?" Adele said.

"Or just funny," Jolene quipped. "Come on, I had to get your attention somehow."

"So you used magic?"

"In a way…" she said, considering her words. "As a ghost I have the ability to use humans to do the things I need them to do. It's hard, just let me tell you, but I do have the power."

"So you're like an evil spirit?"

"I am not evil! Geez, where do you come up with this stuff? It's just part of being paranormal, I guess. And the magic comes in handy, too."

Adele took a moment to let all this sink in, then decided to test her. "Well, that makes sense," she said. "So, if this is all about magic, then I want something magical. I want you to do something for me."

"What?"

"Take me to see my mother."

"Excuse me?" Jolene asked, almost as if she'd been taken aback by the request.

"You know magic, don't you?"

"What does that have to do with anything?"

"It has everything to do with anything," Adele said, frustrated. "Prove to me that you are here as my guide to magic. Prove to me that you are who you say you are. And start by taking me to see my mother."

"I can't do that," Jolene said. "Besides, you should never go home again."

"What are you talking about?"

"Don't you know the saying, 'You can't go home again'?"

Adele shook her head.

"Well, you can't," she said.

"Why not?"

"You just can't," she said.

"But that's what I want," Adele told her. "I want to see my mother."

"That would take me a few days," she said. "I'll have to figure out how. That's complicated. Being a ghost, my powers aren't what they used to be."

Adele considered that.

"Pick something smaller," Jolene said.

Adele thought about it. Then she got an idea. "I want a chocolate chip cookie. A good one, homemade."

Jolene grinned. "That I can do."

Adele couldn't help but smile back but it shouldn't have surprised her when Jolene ordered her out of bed and down the stairs and through the house to the kitchen. There, she pointed at a cookie jar in the pantry.

"Ta da!" she said. "Chocolate chip cookies."

"You've got to be kidding me," Adele said, groaning.

"Seriously, taste them," she said. "They're good."

"I thought you'd conjure them up or something."

Jolene sighed with agitation. "Well, I can't just do any little pony trick you ask. I'm a ghost. I have limited power, okay? I can't just use it up for your whims. Besides, why would you want to use magic for something you can do without it? You're not that lazy, are you?"

Adele just stared at her.

"Take one," she said and grinned.

Adele shrugged and opened the jar, reached in and grabbed a cookie. When she bit into it, it almost melted in her mouth. It was so delicious, like it had just come out of the oven. She moaned with pleasure and Jolene smiled at her.

"Chocolate chip was my favorite, too," she said. "I'd love to have one."

"Why don't you?"

"What's the point? I'm a ghost, remember?"

Adele studied her. "If you're a ghost, then how could you pinch me?"

"Because ghosts can do that," she said. "I had a lot of power when I was alive. I've still got a lot, but it's not as strong now."

Adele nodded and finished off the cookie before reaching for another. "So, what do you want with me?"

Jolene smiled. "I want to show you the magic of magic. That's all. It'd be fun to help someone. Besides, you're a special girl, Adele, and only special girls get to become powerful witches."

"So you want to turn me into a witch?" Adele asked.

Jolene stepped back and studied her. "You're already a witch."

"What?"

She nodded. "You have some power; I can see that, though it's limited. I'd be willing to bet there was someone in your family who had a quite a bit and over the years, it's been forgotten and not tended to. When that happens, it just becomes dormant. Your power is dormant."

"There's no one in my family with any power," Adele said and for a second couldn't believe that she was talking about this with a ghost. It was surreal.

"Yeah, you do," Jolene said. "And when you see your mother, you can ask her about it. It could even be somebody from several generations back. It doesn't really matter who, but it's good to know."

"Okay," Adele said and looked around for a napkin to wipe her hands on. When she looked up, Jolene was no longer there. *Great.* She sighed, found a paper napkin and wiped her hands. As she did so, she took a moment to ponder what just happened. Jolene was real. She was a ghost, but she was real and knowing that she might help her gain some magical powers was very enticing. Anything to break up the monotony of her life at Bancroft House would be a good thing and she might be able to help Cecelia along the way, too. That thought made her smile. But then she realized that she'd better get back to bed before Head Mistress Tanner caught her again.

Home Sweet Home

Jolene didn't make an appearance for almost a week after their talk over cookies. She was gone so long Adele began to wonder if she had just hallucinated the whole thing. Of course, she didn't tell anyone about Jolene and never would. She just hoped that the girl was real and that she, herself, wasn't crazy.

Adele was just finishing her supper when she looked up to see Jolene standing by one of the cooks at the stove. The cook was stirring something in a pot and Jolene was mimicking her. Adele almost cracked up. Jolene grinned at her and walked over and leaned against the table.

"What's up, chick?" Jolene asked.

Adele shrugged and glanced at the cooks.

"No, they can't see me," Jolene said.

Adele muttered, "But they can hear me talking."

"Oh!" Jolene said and waved her hands. Just then, the radio that sat on the counter and was never ever turned on started playing an old Beach Boys song, the one about the old lady from Pasadena. The cooks all glanced at it, then turned back to their work, humming along with the tune.

"That ought to take care of that," Jolene said. "So, what's shaking?"

"Dinner," Adele said.

"Ew," Jolene replied and glanced at the remains of Adele's meal. "That looks gross."

"And it tastes worse," Adele said.

"I never understood why they couldn't feed you girls better," Jolene said.

"What do you mean?" Adele asked. "Did you used to go to school here?"

"Well, duh," Jolene said and pulled at her skirt a little. "Do you really think I wear this to blend in?"

Adele laughed a little. "Well, at least you didn't get stuck with mine."

"Yeah, really," Jolene said. "Wearing that would have turned me into a frickin' poltergeist."

They laughed and Adele said, "So when did you go to school here?"

"It doesn't matter," she replied curtly. "Anyway, are you ready to go?"

"Go where?" Adele asked.

"To see your mother," Jolene said. "Didn't we already have this conversation?"

"I didn't think you were serious," Adele said.

"Well, I was," Jolene replied, then leaned back to study her. "I mean, you do want to go, don't you?"

"I do," Adele said. "But I have to work. After dinner, we have... Well, tonight's dusting night. We have to dust everything in this house."

"You'll be back in plenty of time for that," Jolene said and straightened up, then held out her hand. "Come on. Let's rock and roll."

Adele started to protest, then became oddly excited. She hadn't seen or heard from her mother in months. She was really going to get to see her! Then she thought about that and got some doubts. Was she really going to see her? What if Jolene took her into another dimension and she got stuck there, like in some *Twilight Zone* episode? The thought did frighten her. But then she thought about the cookie experience. What if she just showed her some grainy footage or something? Well, that would certainly be disappointing.

"It's now or never," Jolene said. "Grab onto my hands."

Adele hesitated for a moment, trying to make up her mind whether she wanted to do this or not. Jolene stared at her expectantly. "But you're a ghost," Adele said. "How can I grab hold of your hands?"

"Are you going to do it or what?" Jolene nearly shrieked. "I mean, I can't stop and explain everything single little thing to you. If you want to go, let's go. Now!"

Well, why not? What did she have to lose? Adele nodded and said, "Okay, okay, let's go then."

"Finally," Jolene muttered under her breath, then stopped and listened.

Adele stopped and listened, too. Just then, the song on the radio changed to another, Joan Jett's version of the Runaways classic *Cherry Bomb*. Adele recognized it because her mother was a big Joan Jett fan, which was odd because she was mostly a hippie at heart and loved long dresses, natural remedies and Stevie Nicks. The music must have been too much for Jolene because it totally took her over.

She started lip-syncing the tune and doing rock stances. Adele couldn't help but laugh at her and then join in.

"*Cherry bomb!*" Jolene shouted/sang, then held out her hands. "It's time. Come on!"

Adele jumped into action. She stood up and held out her hands. Jolene grabbed her hands, squeezing them tightly. She didn't know what made her put her trust in her. She just did it even though a flicker of fear begged her to question her decision. She brushed it off and hoped her loyalty would not be repaid by betrayal.

"Three chants," Jolene told her over the music. "Repeat after me."

Adele nodded.

"*Take me away, take me away, take me away far and near, take me away, dear old dear.* Three times, Adele. Three times only."

Adele nodded, then she and Jolene chanted, "*Take me away, take me away, take me away far and near, take me away, dear old dear. Take me away, take me away, take me away far and near, take me away, dear old dear. Take me away, take me away, take me away far and near, take me away, dear old dear.*"

Adele's eyes closed involuntarily as she chanted and then she felt herself move forward but not much. And then she felt herself lift up off the floor. She looked down to see her feet dangling above the floor of the kitchen. Then she glanced over at the cooks, who were still listening to *Cherry Bomb* and were, oddly enough, grooving to it. Adele cracked up. She wondered how the cooks didn't see them, but realized that Jolene had probably cast a spell on them or something. Then it all made sense, all of it. From the book, to the nurse's odd behavior, to the cooks, Jolene had done it all. She wondered why briefly but then, for no reason at all, started laughing. Maybe it was just being in the absurd situation or having the feeling of freedom she was getting from this, but something was making her happy, so happy she forgot about everything else.

"No laughing!" Jolene said. "Oh, no, oh no! Close your eyes!"

Adele squeezed her eyes shut and felt something push her back. She fell back on her bottom and felt her heart start to race. When she opened her eyes, she expected to see the kitchen but instead she and Jolene were sitting on someone's lawn.

"Ow, ow," Adele said and rubbed her bottom.

"You didn't stay concentrated," Jolene told her.

"You're the one who started grooving to the music," Adele said.

"Sorry," Jolene said. "I like music. It moves me."

"That's surprising," Adele said. "I mean, you being a ghost and all."

"Do you think that just because I'm a ghost I don't know or can't remember anything?"

"I hadn't really thought about it, to be honest with you," Adele said.

"Whatever," Jolene said, looking around, then smiled widely. "Well, what do you think?"

"I thought the chant would be fancier," Adele said.

"Fancier?" Jolene asked, rolling her eyes. "Are you serious? What do you want me to do? Say it in Latin?" She shook her head in frustration. "Okay, let's stop for a minute. Lesson number one, the fancier something is, the less likely it will work. Magic isn't that fancy. Magic is mostly a feeling, Adele. Don't forget that."

"And don't force," Adele replied curtly, just to get her.

"Smarty pants," Jolene said. "Well, here you are."

She stepped to the side and waved one arm over a house Adele did not recognize.

"This isn't my house," Adele said, looking at the brick rancher. She looked around the yard, then at the darkening sky above, then at the two new cars in the driveway. Where was this? Why were they here?

"You didn't tell me to take you to your old house," Jolene said. "You said, and I quote, 'Take me to see my mother.' Remember?"

"I know, but she's not here, Jolene," Adele said. "I don't even know this place. I mean, where is this? My mom is at home. She's not here."

"Are you sure about that?" Jolene asked with one raised eyebrow. Then she turned to the big front window. Adele glanced at Jolene then walked to the window. She peered inside. It was a nice house, an older one that looked like it had been recently renovated. The furniture was new and the room clean and comfortable.

As she looked around, she noted that this house probably belonged to a family. There had to be kids because there were a few board games on the coffee table and a video game console sitting next to a huge flat-screen TV, which was perched on a fancy looking credenza. *Nice*, she thought to herself. But what she was doing at this house was beyond her. She was about to turn to Jolene and tell her she'd gotten the wrong house when all of a sudden, she saw someone coming into the room. She ducked down quickly, then inched up to see the person. She almost fell over when she recognized her mother. *What was she doing here?*

She watched her mother as she came into the room and began tidying it up. She picked up books and put them in the bookshelf. She picked up the games and stashed them in the bottom drawer of the credenza. She cleaned the room up, giving it a little dusting with an old cloth as she went.

"You know, I'd be in my thirties now," Jolene said, hunkering down beside Adele "If I were still alive. I'd probably have kids and a husband. Or maybe just kids. Definitely kids. I always wanted a brood."

Adele didn't respond, mostly because her eyes were filled with tears. How could her mother do this to her? To her sisters? To little Cecelia who was so sickly and needed help? She was confused but suddenly became overwhelmed with anger and with hatred. She hated her mother then, hated the fact that she was her daughter, that she'd ever put any trust whatsoever into her. She had moved into a new house where there was plenty of room for all of them and she was keeping it to herself. How could she?

And she wasn't sick! In fact, she looked like the picture of health. Adele was about to stand and confront her when a young girl about her age entered the room. Her mother stopped cleaning, turned to her, smiled and nodded at what the girl was saying. Then a boy came into the room. He was a little older than the girl. They both had dark blonde hair and looked healthy, well-fed, and happy, which was a stark contrast to Adele and her sisters.

Suddenly Adele had some hope. Maybe this wasn't her mother's house after all. This house belonged to someone else. She was probably just the maid or looking after the kids until someone got home. Adele was about to breathe a sigh of relief when a man came into the room, grabbed her mother by the middle and gave her a big hug. She laughed and wriggled away, shaking her head at him playfully. She looked happy. She looked like she was in love. Adele noticed that she was wearing a wedding ring with an engagement ring. Then she knew. Her father had never been able to afford an engagement ring for her mother. She knew what was going on. Her mother had found another family.

Adele recognized the man. His name was Tom Baxter and he'd worked with her father in the mines. He had come over to their house a few times to ask her father questions about an old Camero he was working on. Adele glanced to the side and saw, in addition to the two new cars, an older model Chevy Camero parked under the carport, probably the same one he'd always been bugging her father about. He must have gotten it fixed because it looked almost new.

She pushed the thought out of her head as the realization of what was happening dawned on her. Great! Yet another thing to deal with, to have emotions about. Why couldn't anything ever be easy? Now, on top of everything else, including making contact with a ghost, Adele had to contend with the fact that her mother was never going to come for her and her sisters. She was leaving them at Bancroft House to rot. It was that simple.

"Let's get out of here," Jolene said.

"No," Adele said and looked around, stared at the carport, which was near the back door, then walked over, leaned against the brick wall and set her jaw.

"What are you doing?" Jolene asked. "We have to go!"

"You go," Adele said. "I have to talk to my mother."

"Adele," Jolene said. "That is a bad idea."

"I don't care."

"We can't stay here," Jolene said. "It might be a while before she comes out."

"I'll sit here all night if I have to," Adele said and crossed her arms.

Jolene shrugged and leaned against the wall beside her. They didn't speak for a long few minutes.

"Oh, I can't stand it," Jolene said and waved her arm.

Adele was about to ask her what she was doing when, just then, her mother came out of the back door with a bag of garbage. Adele straightened up and stared her dead in the eye. Her mother stopped short, gasped and held her hand over her heart.

"Adele? What are you doing here?" she asked.

"More like, what are you doing, Mother?" Adele hissed. "Is that your new family or something?"

Her mother sighed, threw the garbage into a large trashcan and walked over to her. "How did you get here?" she asked. "Where are your sisters?"

"What do you care?" Adele snapped.

She jerked back and looked to the side, as if she were trying to form her thoughts into words. She turned back and stared at Adele and said, "I care. I do."

"You have a new family," Adele said, tears streaming down her face. "You left us in that hellhole so you could have a new man and a new family."

"It's not like that," she said, shaking her head. "I was planning on getting you girls after I got the settlement from the mine."

"What are you talking about?" Adele asked.

Her mother stared at her. "Well, if someone dies in a mining accident, like your father did, the mine usually gives the family some money."

"You got money?!" Adele nearly screamed. "And you left us there?"

"Well, it wasn't much, not after I paid some bills and… It just didn't go that far, Adele."

Then Adele realized where the money had gone. It had gone for this nice house, for the two new cars, for the man and the two kids, that's where it had gone! How could she? How could she have done this to her and her sisters?

"You spent it all, didn't you?" Adele asked, almost crying. "That was our money, for our daddy! It was meant for us, wasn't it? And you spent it on yourself and on them!"

"Well, yes, I did," she said, wringing her hands together. "But it's not like that! There is a little left and as soon as I can, I am coming for your girls."

"You're lying," Adele said. "You're never coming for us and you never planned on coming for us! Daddy just died and you've got a new husband and new kids!" She stopped and shook her head. "And Tom Baxter? Daddy was always talking about what an idiot he was!"

"Adele, listen to me," she said. "I married Tom because I had no choice. But I do love him. And I love you and your sisters. I'm working on getting you away from there."

"You're lying," Adele cried. "I know you're lying!"

"I'm not!" she cried, starting to cry. "I am trying, honey, but it's hard. It's hard to bring three kids into a new marriage."

"Especially when there are already two kids, right?" Adele spat. "You picked him over us. You picked his kids over us, too. He doesn't want us, does he? That's why you gave us away!"

"It's not like that," she said again, wiping at her eyes. "It's just hard, okay, Adele? It's just hard to do the things you need to do. To bring it up, to convince someone of something."

"Hard?" Adele spat and held up her hands. "How's this for hard? How's working like a dog every day! How's starving for hard, mother? Oh, yeah, we starve. We don't get that much to eat!"

She looked away. "I don't know what to say. I don't know what to do."

Her mother was weak, she was so weak. Adele understood that now. If she'd had any strength in her at all, she would have never taken them to Bancroft House in the first place. And, chances were, she knew all along what the "work" scholarship was. She was one of those women who had to have a man take care of her at any cost, even her children. She was so pathetic. Adele couldn't stand to look at her and she felt, probably for the first time, hatred for her own mother. She felt it rise up in her and demand attention.

Without thought, Adele raised her hand and was about to throw a simple curse at her she'd learned in the book. It wouldn't have hurt her too much but she'd have gotten the point. But Jolene grabbed her hand and shook her head.

"Don't even *think* about it," she hissed. "Back it down, now."

Adele glared at her but dropped her hand. However, her mother had taken note of her action.

"What are you doing?" her mother asked, her eyes narrowing. "Why did you raise your hand like that?"

Adele set her jaw and refused to answer.

She stared at her and then a look crossed her face as if something had dawned on her. "Oh, God, no. No, Adele. No!"

"No what, mother?"

"That isn't for you," she said. "No one got that in this family. That was your father's side. We don't have it."

"We don't have what?"

"You know damn well what I'm talking about," she said. "You don't want to have anything to do with that stuff, Adele."

"With what stuff, mother?" she snapped.

"It's evil," she shrieked.

"It is not," Jolene scoffed. "Your mother is a real drama queen."

"Well, if you didn't want me to have anything to do with it," Adele told her mother. "Then you shouldn't have dropped me off at a place where there happens to be—"

Her mouth stopped working for a second. She glanced over at Jolene who shook her head, letting her know she'd put a clamp on Adele's mouth and wasn't about to unclamp it. Why had she done this? Adele wanted to shake her. She had so much to say and now she couldn't.

"Do not bring me into this," Jolene said. "I have nothing to do with this."

Adele rolled her eyes and nodded, letting her know she wouldn't say anything about her. Jolene sighed, threw up her hand and unclamped her mouth. Adele turned back to her mother. "It doesn't matter. You go back in there and kiss their butts like you were. You do what you have to do, Mother, and I will do what I have to do."

She turned to leave.

"Don't go fooling with that stuff!" her mother screamed after her.

"What do you care?" Adele screamed back and turned to her.

"I care!" she hollered. "I am your mother and I love you!"

"You know, you're such a good mother. You never even asked me about your other two kids," Adele said. "You can rot for all I care."

"Don't say that to me," she begged. "Adele, I'm trying! I am!"

"You're not," Adele said. "I will never, ever talk to you again. I will find a way to get myself and your other two daughters out of that place. But don't you ever cross my path again, lady. I am done with you."

"Adele, please don't—"

Her mother's mouth suddenly clamped shut. Adele looked over at Jolene, who'd done the same thing to her as she'd done to Adele.

"We have to get going," Jolene said. "Now."

Adele nodded and turned back to her mother, who looked terrified. Well, good enough for her. She started to say something else, but realized she had nothing more to say. The betrayal she'd just experienced was too great for that. She knew now that there was no way out of Bancroft House and that her mother would never come to rescue her or her sisters. It wasn't lost on Adele that she was the one who put them in there in the first place.

She glanced at Jolene. "Can you do something so she'll forget this ever happened?"

Jolene nodded. "Are you sure you want me to?"

Adele nodded. "Please. I don't want her to know I've been here."

"Just do it," Adele said, tears streaming down her cheeks. "Before she says anything else."

Jolene nodded and waved her hand towards Adele's mother. All of a sudden, she straightened up, muttered, "Oh," then turned on her heel and went back into the house. As the door shut, Adele burst into tears. Jolene pulled her close and let her cry on her shoulder for a few minutes, then lifted her face to her.

"We have to go now," Jolene said. "Hang on tight."

Adele wiped her tears, grabbed Jolene's hands and closed her eyes. In a matter of seconds, she and Jolene were back at Bancroft House. It was as if no time had passed.

"She wasn't sick," Adele murmured.

"What?"

"Head Mistress Tanner told me she was sick," she said and turned to her. "She wasn't sick."

Jolene nodded. "I think that's what she tells all the girls once they're admitted to the school. It makes them want to work harder. You know, to help their dear mothers."

Adele stared at her as her words sank in, then she felt her heart sink and she wanted to burst into tears. But she didn't want Jolene to see her cry any more than she already had.

"You made a smart decision about making her forget," Jolene told her.

"Yeah, I guess I did," Adele said, though she wasn't so sure.

The next few days were tough for Adele. Along with all the work, knowing what her mother had done to them was almost too much to bear. The more she thought about it, the more she fumed. She began to go into a downward spiral and feel anxious most of the time. Of course, her sisters noticed but they knew that when she was "in one of her moods" to leave her alone.

Lotta came up to her after class and asked, "What's wrong with you?"

"I just hate this place," Adele replied, refusing to look her in the eye.

"Well, we all do," Lotta said. "But your attitude is making it harder on the rest of us."

"That's true," Jane said, walking up to them. "Girl, you have been acting like a real brat."

"Why don't you leave me alone?" Adele snapped at her. "As I recall, we are not friends."

Jane nodded. "Sorry."

Adele turned to Lotta. "And I can't help it if I wear my feelings on my sleeve. I've been through a lot, okay? Sorry if it's disturbing you."

Lotta nodded, then glanced at Jane and they both turned to leave. Neither one said another word as they walked away. Adele watched them then saw Jolene in the thick of the crowd. Jolene waved to her. Adele glanced around to see if anyone was watching and then followed Jolene out of the house.

"What do you want?" Adele asked her.

"You haven't been studying the book."

"No, and I don't intend to."

"Why not?" Jolene asked.

"Well, my mother told me not to," Adele said. "I think I should take her advice."

"Your mother is a frightened, weak woman," Jolene told her. "Why would you listen to anything she has to say?"

"And why should I listen to you?" Adele snapped.

"Because you should."

"Maybe I don't want to," Adele said. "Maybe I can't help my sisters but maybe I can help myself."

"By doing what?"

"Running away," Adele said.

"That never solves anything."

"I think it might."

"And where would you go?" Jolene said. "I am *so* sure there are *so* many high paying jobs for fourteen-year-old girls."

"I'll be fifteen soon," Adele said.

"Even so, you've got a bright future ahead of you if you leave. I mean, this may suck but being out there in the real world won't be a picnic, either."

"Like I have a bright future anyway!" Adele snapped. "I mean, I have nothing, Jolene. It's all been taken away from me. And I have to work hard every day and it's not right!"

"Yeah, I know," Jolene said. "But there is a way out and it's not by running, Adele."

"And what is it?"

"Magic," Jolene said.

Adele rolled her eyes. "What good is that ever going to do me?"

"You have no clue as to what you're saying," Jolene told her. "You haven't been studying, which means you can't possibly begin to understand what you can do with it. You're being really stubborn—and stupid to top it off."

"So what?!" Adele shouted. "Who cares about me? No one! No one cares about me and never will! Look at what my mother did to me. She brought me and my sisters here and abandoned us!"

"Maybe you were brought here to be who you were meant to be," Jolene said.

"But I'm nobody!" Adele hissed, getting more and more upset. "And nobody cares about me!"

"Don't say that!" Jolene snapped. "Don't you ever put down what you are! You have power and you cannot say otherwise!"

"And how does that help me?" she asked. "How can I get us out of here?"

"Well, there's nothing you can do about it right now," Jolene said. "You can sit around and get angry or you can move on and find a solution to your problem."

"There is no solution!" Adele hollered. "There is no way out of this place!"

"Of course there is," Jolene said. "Think, Adele, think!"

"I need money," she said. "I'm only fourteen and I can't even earn any."

"Sure, you could," she said.

"How?"

"You will find a way," she said.

"How?" Adele said angrily, getting very frustrated at the mind games Jolene seemed to enjoy playing.

"It's called magic," Jolene said.

"Forget you," Adele said. "I mean it, too. Leave me alone and forget about me too while you're at it."

"Listen," Jolene said, regaining some of her lost composure. "Your mother is a weak woman. She is one of those women who has to have someone take care of her. That's all."

"Oh, really?" Adele said, rolling her eyes. "Ya think? She grabbed onto the first man she could and tossed her daughters to the side."

"It's called survival, Adele."

"Well, what about us?" Adele shrieked. "We're not surviving! Look at Cecelia!"

"What about Cecelia?" Jolene asked, getting a concerned look.

"It's just she…" Adele told her. "She's sick. I mean, I know she's sick. The nurse says she's anemic. But I have a feeling she's also got a vitamin deficiency, too. She needs more than she's getting. You know what I mean? I don't know what to do."

"Things will take care of themselves," Jolene said and patted her shoulder. "You shouldn't worry so much."

"I always have," Adele said. "Most of my life."

"And it does you no good," Jolene said. "Don't worry about little Cecelia. It will work out for the best."

Adele stared at her. "If you say so."

"I say so," Jolene said and smiled at her. "Now we need to get back to the book. You need to start practicing. That's the only way to get you where you need to be."

"Let me just ask you this," Adele said. "What good is this going to do me?"

Jolene smiled. "If you can do magic, you can do anything."

Adele stared at her.

"It's time for you to take charge," Jolene said. "No more horsing around. No more getting distracted by situations you have no control over. Nothing but practice. Once you master this, you will become the master of your own universe and, let me just tell you, that's a pretty good feeling."

Adele liked that idea and smiled for the first time in days. "Okay, fine. Let's do it."

And so they did.

Fantasy Into Reality

Over the next few months, Adele would sneak out of class and find Jolene. They'd go to a secluded part of the house, usually the library depending on the day, and practice magic. Jolene told her how to take control of the spells by taking control of her mind.

"It will take you years to have full control," Jolene said one day. "But once you have it, you will be able to command what you want out of life. You will be able to manipulate situations and people."

Adele nodded and really began to understand what she was saying. At that point, she found that she could command things—books, utensils, her toothbrush—to come to her. She was also able to levitate things. She was also gaining more control over situations around the house. She learned to change things by just concentrating on what she wanted. She tried this for the first time at dinner. As one of the other girls gathered her tray to take to the rich girls, she commanded the girl to bring her a plate of food too. She did and from that night on, she ate as the rich girls ate. A few days later, she took it to another level. She went to the door and watched as one of the other girls started to serve the rich girls' dinner. Then she commanded the girl to take a plate over to Cecelia. Cecelia pulled back from it, then looked around confused. She had never gotten a plate like that. Adele concentrated on her and the girls sitting around her and said, "It's yours." And no one took notice. And then she did the same for Eliza. And she did that every night so that they ate well.

And, as her power grew, she was able to do things for all the other girls, too. At least one night a week, she "mixed" up the dinners so that the rich girls were eating the other girls' food and the other girls got the rich girls' food. She also made it so that no one ever knew any differently. And Adele cracked up every time she did it. The rich girls rarely ate anything off their plates anyway, as they were always so concerned with staying thin, but when it was the night to eat the gruel, they *really* didn't eat. This is why she could only risk it once a week. They rarely ate anything and if she did it more often than that, they would have literally wasted away and, inevitably, questions would have started to be asked. But they were so funny to watch whenever she did this.

"Oh, my God," they would say. "What *is* this? It is so gross."

They'd wrinkle their noses and shake their heads and then just sip their milk or water. But not one of them ever complained and not because Adele made sure they didn't. They didn't complain, mostly, because that would have indicated to the other rich girls that they might actually been interested in their food and with eating it. This was not acceptable behavior for them, as they all wanted to stay thin.

Not only that, but Adele made sure to give the other girls special treats from time to time. For instance, whenever Sally would leave the conservatory for a few minutes, Adele would "find" a box of candy bars. And she'd hand them out. The girls would eat the candy and smile, talking about how good it was. And, just before Sally came back in, she'd have all the wrappers gathered up and disposed of. No one ever questioned her; they just ate the candy and were glad to get it. And Adele was happy to give it to them. It might not have been much, but it made a difference in everyone's attitude. And isn't that what chocolate's for?

This made her smile with satisfaction and she began to incorporate magic into other things, like her chores. With the dusting, which she absolutely hated, she began to simply command the dust to disappear. She didn't know where it went, but she'd command it to be gone and then, it would be gone. She'd stand there and pretend to dust when, in actuality, she was going over spells she was learning from the book.

Adele actually began to not mind Bancroft House because of all the things she was learning. As she progressed in her magic, her life began to improve, as did the lives of the other girls. Time actually began to speed up a little as she learned more and more from Jolene. Soon, Thanksgiving was over—Adele was surprised when they were actually served a tasteless but genuine Thanksgiving meal of turkey and dressing—and then it was onto Adele's birthday. She didn't expect anything from anyone but Eliza and Cecelia made her a birthday card and sang *Happy Birthday* to her. That was not only good enough, it was better than enough and Adele appreciated their gesture.

Then it was Christmas and while the rich girls went home for the holidays, most of the other girls stayed and continued their work. But on Christmas Day, Head Mistress Tanner and Ms. Ingles called all the girls down to the library and gave each girl one present. Everyone got a new identical brush and comb set. It wasn't much, but it was something.

And then it was Eliza's birthday in January and then Cecelia's in March. On each of their birthdays, Adele, using magic—and Jolene—to help her, roused them out of bed early, took them downstairs to the kitchen and gave them each a small chocolate cake. Eliza's eyes nearly popped out of her head at the cake and she worried that Adele might get in trouble for baking it in the kitchen. But Adele hadn't baked it. She had summoned it from a bakery close by the school, something that Jolene was teaching her. Adele assured Eliza that it was fine, that no one would ever know and they each had a big slice before Adele sent it away. Cecelia didn't even ask where hers came from and just dove in.

Adele was also able to summon vitamins and iron supplements for Cecelia, which she made her take every day before dinner. She'd pull her to the side and give her the pills with a glass of water. While Cecelia was still weak and needed more than she was getting, it was a start. The main problem that remained was that she couldn't figure out how to explain it to Eliza or Cecelia, or if she should even attempt to. They just took what she gave them without question but as they got older, they'd want to know how she was doing all this. She knew she had to tread lightly and do what she could without *overdoing* it. She didn't want to arouse any suspicion on her or her sisters, so she kept it quiet, doing what she could for them when she could.

During this time, Jolene was showing Adele so many new things she sometimes wondered how she would retain it all. But she was gaining power and she could feel it. She felt it when she summoned Cecelia's vitamins and she felt it when she commanded the roses to de-thorn themselves. She didn't know exactly how it worked or where the vitamins came from, or how the roses got into such a beautiful, perfect state, and she probably never would. But she began to understand that there was a need, a want deep inside of her that made it all possible.

Jolene also taught her many things which weren't even in the book. She said, "You have to make sure that you walk that fine line between reality and fantasy. You don't want to overlap too much."

Adele squinted at her. The sun was bright that day and they were in the back of the house in a little alcove. There were a few rich girls idling around and a few playing tennis on the court just beyond the patio. A few were off to the side lounging around lazily and having the most inane conversation. "My hair is *so* dry," one of them said and began running her hand through it. "I need some new condition or something." Another one chimed in, "I got a new conditioner and it made my hair so *greasy!*" A few of them gasped.

"Oh, my, what a tragedy," Jolene said and laughed a little.

Adele rolled her eyes and was glad they didn't notice her. And they didn't notice them because Jolene had taught her a spell that made her less visible. She wasn't quite invisible, but her aura was minimized so she didn't stick out so much. She simply blended into the background. Since she'd learned the spell, she'd been able to be wherever she wanted to pretty much all the time. She *loved* that spell.

"But, as I was saying," Jolene said. "It's important to really keep an eye on what is in your fantasy world and what is in your real world."

"What do you mean?" Adele asked.

"Just use your mind…"

"I don't understand."

"If you let fantasy take over your world," she said. "Then that's all it will ever be. You have to know when to not cross the line from fantasy to reality. Fantasy had its place but reality is a constant. The trick is to turn your fantasy into reality."

"Yeah," Adele said. "Like my fantasy about leaving here."

"Right," Jolene replied. "That's nowhere near being a reality. You have to find a way to step back and allow your fantasy to form without actually being involved with it."

Adele thought about that. If they were to ever leave, they would have to have money and lots of it. But how could she get her hands on any money? Jolene nodded when she told her this.

"Yes, money does make a difference," she said. "But how are you going to get enough money to leave? And you can't just leave. You're underage. They will track you down and bring you back here. "

"I don't care. I have to do it. I have to leave. I have to do it for my sisters."

She nodded. "I never had a sister. I always wanted one, though."

Adele stared at her, wondering if she was hinting she'd like to be her sister. But she knew better. Jolene wasn't emotional like that.

"If I only had a little money like the rich girls," Adele said, thinking about it. "It would be so easy."

Jolene studied her. "You're obsessed with the rich girls." She smiled slyly at her and sang, "'*You're a rich girl, and you've gone too far 'cause…*'" She trailed off, humming the tune.

"What's that?"

"It's a song, Hall and Oates," Jolene replied. "It was one of my mom's favorite songs."

Adele stared at her as she continued to hum the tune. Then she shook herself and said, "I am not obsessed with the rich girls."

"Oh, you are," she replied, nodding. "When you see someone that you think has it so much easier than you, you start thinking about what it would be like. You're jealous. With magic, that's dangerous. You have to learn to pull back from that sort of envy. You have to be able to be strong enough to form your own world and not worry about someone else's."

"Okay," Adele said. "But they do have it easy."

"Maybe they do and maybe they don't," Jolene said. "On the surface, a lot of people look like they've got it easy. But if you dig a little deeper, you'd see that most don't have it as easy as you'd like to imagine."

She pointed to a rich girl playing tennis with another. "She comes from an abusive home. That's one reason she's in here. And that one," she said and pointed to one sitting by herself by a tree. "She has emotional problems brought on by spending most of her time in boarding schools. She feels unwanted and unloved most of the time."

"How do you know this?" Adele asked.

"I read people," Jolene said. "And I snoop. Do you honestly think all I do around here is teach you magic? Oh, no. I listen to the rich girls as much as the other girls. And they've got problems, too."

"So, what's her deal?" Adele asked and pointed to the rich girl who had tripped her.

"She's just a spoiled brat," Jolene said and laughed. "But anyway, one thing you never need to get too far away from is empathy. Once you start thinking you're the only one in the world with some sort of problem, you begin to tread into dangerous territory. Empathy will enable you to really get into other people's heads and to really understand situations. This is very important for a witch. That's our biggest job and that's why you have to learn to read situations and people until it becomes second nature."

"I get that," Adele said. "And how do I do it?"

"Just by closing off your mind to yourself and your problems and really feeling someone else's presence," she said. "If you can do that, you can master anything."

"I'll give it a try," she said. "But I do wish I could start earning some money for us."

"Maybe you'll get to," Jolene said. "Put it out there and see what happens."

"But how am I going to be able to do that?" Adele said.

"By stopping getting hung up on trying to force things into being," Jolene said. "This is your biggest issue, Adele. You are such a control freak. Stop doing that. Stop forcing. Just allow. Allow."

Adele tried to do just that but still didn't get how it was going to work out. However, the opportunity seemed to just drop into her lap a few days later. Mr. Adams had two small sons. They occasionally came to the school with him and attempt to wreck the place. One day, they were tearing through the hall and ran right into Adele. They were cute, small boys and she couldn't help but smile at them.

"Whoa," she said. "Where are you two going in such a hurry?"

"The train's coming!" one of them hollered excitedly.

"Oh, no!" Adele said, playing along. "Where is it?"

"There!" the other one screamed and pointed to an imaginary train.

Just then, Mr. Adams ran up and, once he saw his sons with Adele, stopped. "Thank God," he said. "I thought they'd made a run for it."

"No," Adele said. "They're fine."

"Thanks, Adele," he said and took their hands and started to walk off.

Jolene strolled up to Adele and whispered in her ear, "Put it in his mind," she said. "Tell him you can help babysit his kids."

Adele stared at her, then back at him. But before she could speak, he held up his hand.

"Adele," he said. "Is there any way possible that you might be interested in a little babysitting from time to time?"

Adele smiled. "Sure."

"Well, that was easy," Jolene said.

So, on Saturday night, Mr. Adams picked Adele up, took her to his beautiful home about ten miles away and she babysat so he and his wife could have a date night. The two small boys, named Jimmy and Johnny, kept her running almost all night. Jolene sat by and watched. They crashed through her several times and she called them "cretins" and threatened to put a curse on them.

"Which curse?" Adele asked her, laughing.

"The 'sit still or else' curse," she said as they boys ran through her again. "I can't take it!"

Adele laughed as she disappeared, then turned her attention to the boys. She allowed them to pay and wreak havoc for a while longer before finally getting them off to bed around nine and then she and Jolene waited for Mr. Adams and his wife to come home. Once they got there, Jolene said, "Now. Get paid."

"I plan on it," Adele said.

"No," Jolene said. "Make them pay you what this was worth."

"What?"

She rolled her eyes with impatience. "Just tell them to... You know, do whatever you want them to do. With your mind."

Adele stared at her and then realized what she was telling her to do. Her heart began to beat wildly in her chest. Did she dare? Was it possible? As Mrs. Adams chatted about their night and how were the boys and all that, she pulled out a crisp one-hundred dollar bill from her wallet and handed it to Adele. "Here you are, dear. And thank you so much. We haven't been out in ages because, well, we can't get anyone to watch the boys. They are quite rambunctious."

"That's an understatement," Jolene said.

Adele nodded, staring at the money. She hadn't even had the time to insinuate anything but she got paid well nevertheless. That was strange.

"But, anyway, thank you so much," Mrs. Adams continued. "How about next week, too?"

Adele smiled. "That would be great."

She nodded. "Now get going. Our driver will take you home."

Adele nodded. "Have a good night."

"You too, dear," she said.

After Adele got back to the school, she began to feel guilty.

"What's wrong?" Jolene asked.

"I feel kind of guilty," Adele said. "And the thing is, I didn't do anything. She just handed me the money."

"For those two hooligans, that's a bargain," Jolene said. "But you did do something. You did a really good job with those kids. And you probably deserved a lot more."

"Oh," Adele muttered.

"Are you seriously feeling guilt over getting paid well?" Jolene said. "Let me tell you one thing about guilt, Adele, it has no place in a witch's mind. Get rid of it. Guilt will trip you up more than anything else. Besides, what's a hundred bucks? They were gone a really long time, too. Also, when does he ever pay you for working in his flower factory?"

"You're right," Adele said and felt the guilt dissipate. "Now I feel like Robin Hood!"

"I wouldn't go that far," Jolene said, laughing. "But, yeah, get used to that feeling and when the time comes to really use your powers of insinuation, you will be able to do it. Feel good that you have power. Don't ever feel bad about your power."

"Okay," Adele said.

And so, her babysitting job became an almost weekly thing. She knew if she could keep this up, when it was time to leave, she'd have quite a bit of money saved. And that was a good feeling.

As she got better at magic, as she advanced, her attitude began to change. She was becoming not only physically stronger due to the better meals, but she was becoming mentally stronger as well. And with this new mental strength, she began to redefine herself. She realized her time at Bancroft House wasn't going to last forever and that soon, she and her sisters would have to leave and they'd really be on their own. Once that day came, she wanted to be ready to take care of herself and Eliza and Cecelia. She knew the day was approaching and she was just hoping to hold on until she was ready to get out into the world and become what she was meant to become. She was still a little fuzzy on that. But the day when they'd all say goodbye to that awful place was coming soon and Adele couldn't wait. In fact, she had already begun counting down the days till their departure.

But it came a little earlier for someone else.

Cecelia's Friend

Every spring, Bancroft House held a lavish banquet for all their benefactors. These were people who contributed to the school to keep it going, usually alumnae and parents of alumnae. The house was buzzing with activity and the other girls were kept busy helping with the preparations. The entire house was cleaned and straightened, though it didn't need it because they kept it very tidy most of the time anyway. The dining room was readied by clearing out all the tables and bringing in big, round ones which were covered with white linen, gleaming China and sparkling silverware. The whole place was decorated with pretty streamers and big, tropical plants. On each table sat a beautiful flower arrangement that the other girls had painstakingly put together.

During all of this, Head Mistress Tanner walked around and supervised, making sure everything was perfect. She rode the girls hard, yelling at them if a flower arrangement was a little askew or a cobweb was found in a far corner of the house. This seemed to go on forever and by the time the banquet rolled around, the girls were so exhausted, they almost fell into bed.

But not so for Lotta, Jane, Eliza and Adele, who were asked to serve. Adele was very surprised at this because she hadn't been allowed near the rich girls since she'd had the altercation with that one. Even so, she put on the black uniform and the black shoes and pulled her hair back. She and Eliza went down to the dining room by themselves and were joined a little later by Lotta and Jane, who was having a hard time getting her hair under control.

"It has a mind of its own," she said and shook the thick ponytail. "Once it gets warm and the humidity rises, watch out! Kaboom!"

Adele nodded at her but made no attempt to laugh at her lame joke. That's the way it had been between them since that night in the kitchen and she had no intention of ever letting Jane back into her life. Jane stared at her with a hurt expression, then shrugged it off.

Eliza just stared at her, then glanced at Adele and then she turned away, giving Adele the feeling that she thought she should make up with Jane. However, because she was so quiet and didn't like to cause any trouble, she wouldn't come out and say anything. Which was fine with Adele. She didn't need someone else telling her to do something she didn't want to do. Therefore, she ignored her and turned to Lotta. "So, what do we have to do?"

"Serve," Head Mistress Tanner said, entering. "Girls I need you each on a station. You take breads, Lotta. Jane, you will do meats. And Adele, you can do drinks. Oh, oh, Eliza? I want you out front to do coat check."

Eliza nodded and disappeared out of the room while the rest of them went to their stations behind the buffet table. Soon, people were lined up. Adele loved smelling the rich foods that were being served. There was such an abundance, she was almost tempted to grab a plate and go through the line herself. She didn't, though, and smiled and served tea, soda and water. A bartender was also stationed behind a small bar in a corner of the room serving drinks for the grownups. Adele noticed that line was really long.

The night wore on and by the time everyone was served, she was about to fall over from exhaustion. She sighed, leaned against the back wall and closed her eyes momentarily. Then she heard laughter, children's laughter. She looked over and stared across the room at two little girls playing. One was a little blonde girl whom she'd served a soda to earlier, along with her parents. The other little girl, though… She froze. It was Cecelia. Without thinking, Adele ran over, determined to get her back to bed before anyone noticed her, and took Cecelia by the arm.

"What are you doing here?" she asked her. "You need to get back upstairs!"

"Hey, you," the little girl said and gave her a slight shove. "Leave us alone."

"She needs to go back upstairs," Adele said.

"No, don't take her," the little girl said. "We're playing."

She emphasized *playing* as if it were the most important thing in the world. If Adele hadn't been so frightened by what would happen to Cecelia if she got caught playing with one of the patron's children she would have laughed.

"But she has to go back to bed," Adele said and stared at the pretty child. "What's your name?"

"Mabel," she said.

Adele couldn't help but smile, even if she was afraid for Cecelia. She's known a few old ladies in West Virginia who had been named Mabel, but never anyone this young. Somehow, though, the name fit the little girl. It was cute. But now she had to get Cecelia back to bed pronto.

She was about to take her out of the room when, just then, Mabel's mother walked up and smiled at them. "And what are you young ladies doing?"

Adele stared at her. The woman was literally dripping in jewels. She had never seen so many sparkly things in her life. She was wearing diamond earrings and a large emerald ring along with a diamond bracelet and necklace. She was dressed in a beautiful, well-fitting black cocktail dress and smelled of expensive perfume. She reeked of wealth and privilege. Even so, she seemed like a nice person. Adele was very impressed by the way she looked.

"Nothing, Mommy," Mabel said. "We were playing and she made us stop." She gave Adele a bitter look and pointed at her.

Adele wanted to smile but was still too on edge. She and Cecelia could get into some major trouble over this.

"Oh, it's fine," the woman said and smiled at Adele, then at Cecelia. "And this is your sister?"

"It is," Adele said. "This is Cecelia."

"Oh, I love that name," she said. "She's so beautiful."

"Uh huh," Adele said.

"Oh, Mabel likes her," she said. "She doesn't take to many other children. She's an only child."

"Oh?" Adele said.

"Um hum," she replied and studied Cecelia and Mabel, who'd gone back to playing. "She really does like Cecelia, though. It's a miracle! Perhaps Mabel isn't a lost cause."

"Excuse me?"

"Oh, it's just she had trouble at school, getting along sometimes, you know, *with others.*" She paused and continued to stare at the children. "I know it's because we've spoiled her. It's our fault, my husband's and mine. But we do the best we can, you know? It's not my fault she doesn't have a sibling, Lord knows we've tried."

She gave the woman a small smile and said, "Yes, ma'am, but she needs to get back to bed."

The woman nodded, taking no notice of what Adele was suggesting. She sighed and said, "Just let them play. It will keep Mabel busy. Besides, Mabel gets very antsy at these things. Our babysitter cancelled at the last minute."

"Uh, well," Adele said, knowing she couldn't allow Cecelia to stay and play. If Head Mistress Tanner caught her, she'd be in trouble. And Cecelia, still weak and underfed, couldn't handle any sort of physical punishment. Adele was about to just take her out of the room when the head mistress strolled up.

"Oh, hello, Mrs. Vann," she said. "And how are you?"

"Wonderful, Ms. Tanner," she said. "Oh, it's alright if Cecelia stays up and plays with Mabel, isn't it? Her sister is concerned."

"Of course, it's fine," Head Mistress Tanner said, giving Mrs. Vann a warm smile before turning to Adele and giving her a look that let her know that it wasn't alright but she was letting it slide this one time.

"Good, good," Mrs. Vann said. "Oh, while you're here, let me bend your ear on a few issues I have."

"Certainly," she replied and moved aside so Mrs. Vann could pass her. Before she turned to leave, she gave Adele another look and jerked her head back to the buffet table. Adele nodded and went back to her station, watching the two girls play. She had to smile at them. They were having a great time. At one point, they made their way over to get a drink.

"Only one," Adele told Cecelia and handed her a cup full of soda.

"Mmmm, good," Cecelia said, taking a sip. "I love this stuff!"

Adele laughed then remembered that it had been a long time since she'd had any of it, which probably wasn't that bad of a thing.

"Adele," Cecelia whispered. "Can I have a cookie?"

"I don't think so," Adele whispered back. "You need to get back to bed."

"Here," Mabel said, shoving a cookie into Cecelia's hand.

"Thanks," Cecelia said and took a big bite. "Good!"

Adele shrugged and hoped the head mistress didn't chew her out over this. But what could she do? The woman had insisted Cecelia play with her child and wherever there were children at play, there was usually a cookie involved.

Adele shook her head, turned around and nearly jumped out of her skin when she saw Jolene sitting on a chair behind the table. She was reading a book, which was something she did from time to time when she wanted to expend the energy to do so. "But it has to be a really, really good book," she explained and said that it was one of her favorite activities and did make the time go quicker. So, whenever she could get her hands on a book—literally—she took full advantage. Adele studied the cover of the book, then the title: *A Confederacy of Dunces*. Jolene glanced up at her and grinned.

"What 'cha doin'?" Jolene said.

"What are you reading?" Adele had to ask, albeit it quietly. She did not want anyone here thinking she was talking to herself.

Jolene glanced at the cover of the book, then back at her. "*A Confederacy of Dunces*. Won the Pulitzer Prize. Not that you'd know anything about stuff like that."

Adele just stared at her, realizing that the book was probably being suspended in air as no one could see Jolene but herself. She muttered, "Good grief."

"What am I supposed to be reading?" she asked smartly. "*Jackie and Boyfriend?*"

"Put it down," Adele hissed. "People will notice it."

Jolene rolled her eyes then threw the book to the side.

"You need to go," Adele whispered. "I can't talk right now."

"Sure you can," she said, then glanced at Cecelia. "She is going to town on that cookie. Get her another one."

"I can't do that," Adele hissed. "Now leave before someone thinks I'm talking to myself."

She glanced over at Jane who was, in fact, studying her with a raised eyebrow.

"Ah, everyone thinks you're crazy anyway," Jolene said and stood, coming to stand beside Adele at the table. "Big crowd out there. Bigger than last year, that's for sure."

Adele nodded but didn't answer.

"Oh, I wanted to know if you were working on that spell," Jolene said.

"Which one?" Adele muttered looking down.

"I like to call it the 'hat spell'," she said. "But it's really not about a hat, as you can imagine."

"Oh, the beckoning spell," Adele muttered under her breath. "Where you beckon something from another room?"

"Or someone's pocket," she said. "Or their head. Like a hat."

"I've been doing that for months," Adele said. "You know that."

"Well, I want to see it," Jolene said. "Give it a try."

"Here?" Adele almost shrieked, covering her mouth. "No way!"

"Yes, way. See that old man over there?" she asked and pointed. "I want you to beckon his wallet."

"No!"

"Yes," she said. "We're going to put it back. I just want to see how good you are at this. And if you don't want to mess with his wallet, that old woman over there just put her earnings into her bag. They were too heavy for her lobes. Just beckon one. And they're costume jewelry, so don't get excited."

"I am not going to do that," Adele muttered. "Now leave."

"Now do it and I will," Jolene said. "I need to make sure of something."

"Of what?"

"That you can actually do this with real people," she said. "Real people that you could possibly interact with."

"Why?" Adele asked.

"It just changes the dynamics of it, that's all," Jolene said, getting exasperated. "Good grief, just do it!"

Adele knew she wouldn't leave until she did as she asked. She would do this. She would pop up in class or when she was in the flower factory or even brushing her teeth and tell her to try out a spell. One day, she'd been in bed when she had shown up and had forced her to give all the girls a dream containing laughter. The whole room got so rowdy with giggles, Ms. Ingles had barged in, thrown on the lights and chewed them out. Unfortunately for her, there were no privileges the other girls had to take away, so their punishment was to just stop laughing. This was, more or less, fitting of the place.

"Fine," Adele said and concentrated on the old woman's handbag. She envisioned the earrings, though she hadn't actually seen them, and then imagined seeing them through the bag. Soon enough, they were in her mind's eye and all she had to do was call them.

"*Come to me*," she whispered and closed her eyes, then opened her hand. A moment later, a big, rather tacky looking crystal earring was sitting in her hand. She held it up to Jolene, who nodded with approval, then sent it back. "*Go back.*"

The earring disappeared from her hand and back into the old ladies bag.

"Now leave me alone," Adele said.

"You're getting good," Jolene said. "I'm proud of you."

"Well, thanks," Adele said. "Now leave."

"Fine!" she hissed and winked, crossed her arms like Jeanie from *I Love Jeanie*, nodded her head once and disappeared. Despite herself, Adele couldn't help but smile then looked up to see Jane staring at her with an odd look. She didn't give her a second thought and turned to see Eliza making her way across the room towards her. As she came over, Eliza glanced over and saw Cecelia playing with Mabel and held her hands up as if to ask, "What's up with that?"

"I'll explain it later," Adele said as she approached the table. "What do you want?"

"Head Mistress Tanner wants you at coat check with me," she said. "People are starting to leave and it's getting really busy."

"Great," Adele muttered.

"Why is Cecelia over there?" she asked.

"She just came down here for some reason," Adele said. "I guess she got lonely without either of us in the room with her. But, anyway, that little girl started playing with her and then the head mistress said it was fine and here we are."

"We should get her back to bed," Eliza said.

"That's a good idea," Adele said. "You do that and I'll start on the coat check."

Eliza nodded, hurried to Cecelia and had to basically force her out of the room. Mabel started howling and her parents raced over, picked up her and took her out of the room. Adele felt bad, but ignored them and hurried to the coat check which was a small table set up in front of one of the big, first floor hall closets. As soon as she got there, people began to pile in wanting their coats. She hurried and tried her best to keep up with them, then stopped and thought, *Why not use a little magic?*

And with that, she called upon magic to find the coats quickly and by the time Eliza got back downstairs, she had pretty much cleared the crowd.

"Wow, where did everyone go?" Eliza said.

"Home," Adele answered with a slight smile.

Eliza looked around and then turned back to Adele with a sneaky look. "Let's go get a piece of that chocolate pie."

Adele nodded. "That sounds great."

Eliza grinned and headed into the dining room. Adele was about to follow her when Mrs. Vann entered carrying a still crying Mabel.

"Oh, I'm sorry she got so upset," Adele said. "Do you have your ticket?"

Mrs. Vann smiled and handed her the coat check ticket. After Adele retrieved their coats, she smiled at her. "Adele, how old is Cecelia?"

"She just turned seven," Adele said.

"Umm..." Mrs. Vann said. "I noticed she looked a little... How shall I put this? Not very well."

"She's anemic," Adele said.

"Oh, that's what it is," Mrs. Vann said. "Well, tell her we hope she gets to feeling better."

"I will," Adele said and smiled at her. "You have a nice night, ma'am."

"You, too," she said and carried Mabel out.

Adele stared after them then heard Eliza whispering something to her. She turned to see her holding up a whole French silk chocolate pie and two spoons. Adele grinned. Maybe this was good sign. Chocolate pie? Nice people? Yeah, maybe things might be looking up.

And they might not.

It was about a week later when Adele got the news. She'd noticed that Cecelia was being called out several times from work and class to go see the nurse and the head mistress. While she thought this was odd, she hoped that they were finally going to do something about her anemia and the reason probably was because of Mrs. Vann, who did seem very concerned.

Then one day, Cecelia was called out from class and she didn't return. Adele started to get antsy wondering what was going on and was about to go find her when Mr. Adams entered, pointed at Adele and Eliza and beckoned them out of the room.

They immediately jumped up and followed him to Head Mistress Tanner's office. And that's when Adele got a feeling of dread. Once they sat down, they were told that Cecelia had been adopted by Mr. and Mrs. Vann.

At first, the news didn't sink in. And it didn't sink in because Adele knew they still legally belonged to their mother. Her mother hadn't signed them away that she knew of. Or had she? Oh, God, no. She remembered Head Mistress Tanner telling her that her mother had "sold" them to her. Please, God, no. The thought was unbearable.

"Yes, she did," the head mistress said. "She gave up her parental rights the day she left you here."

Eliza grabbed Adele's hand and squeezed so hard it left a bruise. But Adele didn't care. The news that her baby sister had been taken from her was too much to bear. How could she accept this? She didn't think she could, even though she knew it was completely out of her hands.

"You can't do that," Adele said. "We're sisters. We belong together."

"Sometimes this happens," the head mistress said, then glanced at Mr. Adams.

"That's right, girls," Mr. Adams said. "And the Vann's are wonderful people. She will have a great life."

"Where is she?" Adele said.

"She's changing into a new outfit," Head Mistress Tanner said. "She will leave with two colleagues of the Vann's and go to her new home. She'll be settled in nicely by tonight and start her new life tomorrow."

"She won't go," Eliza said. "She can't go. She will have a fit. You don't know her."

"Well, she was quite happy when she learned that she was going to a new home," the head mistress said.

Adele thought about it, then realized what was really going on. The Vann's only wanted Cecelia as a friend for their child, a playmate. Adele could see that. She could see it so clearly. The fear was that she would be worse off than she was now. She was afraid that they might abuse her or that they might ignore her or punish her or neglect her. Cecelia was so small, so fragile, Adele couldn't let that happen.

However, she didn't say anything and tried to recall a spell that might reverse all of this. But her mind was so frazzled with this news she couldn't think straight. What was she going to do? What was she going to do? Panic was setting in and her mind began to race. A lump formed in her throat. This was worse than the day her mother had left them. She couldn't tolerate the thought of being separated from her sister.

"Now," Mr. Adams said. "Let's go say goodbye. And, girls, don't cry in front of her. You'll only upset her."

They were both so shocked they could do nothing but do as he said. They followed him out into the hall and waited until Cecelia, dressed in a new pink sundress and sandals and looking so cute it hurt, came down the stairs. She was followed by two men in black business suits. They weren't colleagues of Mr. Vann's; they were bodyguards. Who were these people who needed bodyguards? And why did they send them to pick her up? She would be terrified.

Adele ran up to her and grabbed her into a big hug then whispered, "If you don't want to go, let me know. I can stop this."

"No," she whispered back. "I want to go. I hate it here."

Adele pulled back and studied her. Was she serious? She glanced at the two men who were waiting. Eliza came up and gave Cecelia a quick hug, then stepped back. Adele couldn't let go. She just couldn't.

"Please, let me go," Cecelia whispered. "Adele, just let me go."

Adele was in shock. She couldn't believe Cecelia wanted to leave.

"Adele," Mr. Adams said. "It's time."

Adele couldn't answer and clung on even tighter to her little sister.

"Now, Adele," Mr. Adams said.

Adele started to cry. She shook her head and said, "You can't take her."

"Let her go, Adele," Eliza said and tried to pry her off Cecelia, who was beginning to shake with fright.

"No!" she screamed. "She's our sister! We can't let them take her!"

Eliza stared at her but didn't answer. Sobs overtook Adele until her voice went dry. She could no longer speak and just held onto Cecelia for dear life.

"Just take her," Mr. Adams told the men.

Adele wasn't sure what they were going to do. Then they pulled Adele off of Cecelia, then took her by the hand and led her away. She watched them take her out of the house through the big front door and put her into a limousine. She watched as Cecelia left her life, probably for good. Then she was gone. Once the car had left, Adele jumped up and ran out of the house, down the lawn and found a tree to lean against. She pulled her knees to her chest and put her head on her knees and sobbed. She didn't know how long she sat there like that but when she looked up, Eliza was next to her.

"It's okay," Eliza said. "She's gone to a better home, Adele. You have to understand that."

While Adele was always high on emotion, Eliza was always high on logic. She was probably the most level-headed human Adele had ever known or would ever know. She accepted things and then she moved on. If she felt any emotions, she kept them to herself until she got them under control. Adele wished she could be more like that but she just wasn't.

"You're probably next," Adele told her. "Some family will come and get you and I'll be all alone."

Eliza just laughed and said, "They're not going to want me, sis. They only wanted her 'cause she's so little and cute."

"I'm sorry I couldn't stop them," she said.

"How could you have?" Eliza sighed and took her hand. "Adele, you're too pig-headed. Daddy always said that. You have to learn to let things go."

"They took her!"

"To a better place!"

"To be that girl's new friend!"

"So? She's going to have her own room and a nanny! I mean, come on, Adele! Somebody actually wants her! I would go with them in a heartbeat to get out of this hellhole. Wouldn't you?"

Adele shrugged. "But she's our sister."

"And we will see her once a month. They promised."

"Just you wait and see," she told her. "I bet we never see her again. Just like Mom."

"Well, I don't know about you, but I will leave here one day and I will see my sister again. It might take me years, but it will happen. I'm surviving this place, Adele. I reckon you should do the same."

Adele nodded. She was going to get out of that place, come hell or high water. And she was going to get her sister back. She was about to tell Eliza this when she saw Jolene coming up the hill towards them. She stared at her, then at Eliza who was back to her usual quiet self. Jolene sat down beside Adele and glanced at Eliza.

"She's taking the news okay," she told her.

Adele didn't answer.

As if on cue, Eliza stood and said, "I better get back. I'll tell them that you're still crying."

Adele nodded.

"See you later," Eliza said and left them staring after her.

"She's very smart," Jolene said. "I like Eliza."

"Yeah," Adele replied.

"Don't worry about Cecelia," Jolene said. "Those people are good people. I made sure of that."

Adele nodded in agreement until her words sank in, then she narrowed her eyes at her and said, "What do mean?"

"Nothing," she said. "I just mean, she's got a good home now. They'll make sure she gets the medical attention she needs. Those people are beyond rich. They probably even have a doctor on staff or something."

Adele stared at her then it dawned on her. "You did this!"

Jolene shrugged. "Maybe."

"Why?" Adele cried. "Why would you do this?"

"Cecelia was too much of a distraction," Jolene said. "You worry about her too much. Besides, this place wasn't good for her."

Adele was too shocked to reply.

"Now, we can really focus," Jolene said.

"I can't believe you," Adele said. "I can't believe you!"

"Well, believe me," Jolene said.

"Why?" Adele asked.

"That child was sick," Jolene told her. "And she was going to get even sicker. This place didn't care about her. She needed a new home and she got one of the best. She basically hit the jackpot."

"I was helping her!" Adele cried. "I was getting her the iron supplements and the vitamins and I was—"

"You were what?" she asked, cutting her off. "What were you doing that could have saved her? An iron supplement here and there wasn't going to help a kid who is made to stand on her feet all day long and work like a dog! She was too little for that! Soon enough, she was going to break and once she did, Adele, there would be no getting her back. It wasn't fair to keep her here when someone out there wanted her and wanted to help get her health back."

"They only wanted her to be their daughter's friend!"

"Did you ever think Cecelia might need a friend, too?" she said, shaking her head. "What about her? There aren't any kids around her age here. She was alone most of the time. She needs to be around kids her own age."

"I can't believe you," Adele said, refusing to see any logic in what she was telling her. "How did you do it? Magic?"

"Actually, no," Jolene said. "I just told Cecelia that her sister needed her. So, she went downstairs. Then I told her that the little girl was lonely and she should go say hello. And so she did. There was no magic to it. It was mostly just plain old manipulation."

"So, she can see you? Cecelia?" Adele asked.

Jolene nodded. "Little kids usually can. She probably just thought I was a rich girl. I don't think she understood I'm a ghost or anything."

"I still can't believe you," Adele said, shaking her head.

"Listen, I just read the situation, like I've been telling you to do," Jolene said. "The woman was desperate for another child; the kid wanted a sister; Cecelia needed a good home. And the father… The father could have cared less and just wanted to make them happy. I didn't use magic. I just brought them all together."

"You are an awful human being," Adele said, fuming.

"I'm a ghost, but still," Jolene said.

"She was my family," Adele said.

"She still is," she replied.

"How could you do that to us?" Adele asked, shaking her head. "She's our sister!"

"It's called survival," Jolene said. "We talked about this."

"I can't believe you! You set this up!"

"That kid needed a better home than this," Jolene said. "You have to admit that. You need to stop being selfish and think of her."

"No, I don't," Adele said. "I don't!"

"Well, you should," Jolene said.

"Whatever," Adele said and began to fume. "You will have to make this right."

"I will?" Jolene asked and almost laughed.

"Yes, you will," Adele said and stared sideways at her. "You will take me to see her."

"What?"

"Take me to see her," she demanded.

"No! Look at what happened with your mother."

"If you don't take me," Adele said, standing. "I will not do magic with you anymore."

"Well, you're so far into it, it's no longer a choice, Adele," Jolene said and stood up next to her. "Magic is now a part of who you are. You couldn't stop doing it if you wanted to."

She was right. Adele knew this, too. She knew she was gaining power as a witch. But she wasn't at the level to go visiting her sister just yet. She would be there someday, but not yet. She still needed Jolene for that.

"Take me to see her," Adele hissed and got in her face. "I want to see how she's going to live."

"No," Jolene said. "Now back off."

"Now!" Adele yelled. "I mean it."

She was getting aggressive. Her grief was getting the best of her and she felt so out of control. Jolene wasn't having it. She grabbed her arm and hissed, "Stop it."

Adele knew it drained her when she did this. Anytime she touched her, she could feel the power draining from Jolene. Adele wanted to drain her power, her energy. She wanted to take it all from her. She was so infuriated that she would have fought her if she hadn't been a ghost.

"Who are you to interfere with my life?" she asked her. "How dare you?"

"Now you're going to listen and you're going to listen good," Jolene said. "I will only say this once. Cecelia was sick. She was getting sicker. These awful people who run this place could have cared less. Now she is with a good family that will take care of her. This is the best thing for her. If you can't get that through your thick skull, you're in trouble. There is nothing you could have done for her."

"I could have used magic to fix her," Adele said.

"Really?" Jolene asked. "You're a healer?"

"What's that?"

Jolene scoffed, "Obviously something you're not, Adele. Now let it go."

She released her arm and Adele took a breath. "You have to let me talk to her," she said pitifully. "Please, Jolene. It's important. I just need to see that she's okay and happy and I'll be over it."

Jolene rolled her eyes.

"So, you're not going to do it?" Adele asked, already knowing the answer to her question.

Jolene shook her head. "It's too risky."

"Fine," she replied and started off. "Just leave me alone then."

"Okay, fine," Jolene called after her. "I guess I could take you to see her. But not now. Not anytime soon. She has to get acclimated and if you storm into her life right now, you're just going to upset her."

Adele stopped and turned around. "When can you take me?"

"Well, I need more power, so it could take a few weeks," Jolene said. "But if I do this, I need something in return this time."

"What are you talking about?"

"There is something I've been wanting," she said. "You can help me."

"Really?"

"Yes," she said empathically. "If you help me, I might help you."

"But you're the reason I have to do this," Adele said. "Besides, it's easy for you."

"It's not that easy."

"It is that easy," Adele told her.

"Okay, fine. So, what's in it for me?"

"What do you mean?"

"I mean," Jolene said, sitting on the grass and tucking her legs under her. "If I do you a good deed, then you do me one."

"What do you want?"

"There's something in the school safe," she said. "Something that was taken from me."

"What is it?"

"It doesn't matter," she replied, shaking her head with impatience. "All that matters is that you get it for me and, maybe, I'll take you to see your sister."

"But it's in a safe!" Adele cried. "A safe is locked. I don't know the combination."

"I do."

If she knew the combination, why didn't she just get it herself? Jolene gave her a look. *Oh.* Adele stepped back and stared at her, wondering why Jolene always had to go through riddles to get what she wanted. Then she realized why. Jolene couldn't physically open the lock but she didn't want to come out and say that. Well, that made sense.

"I can't do it," Adele said. "I can't. If I got caught, they'd probably flog me or kick me out or something."

"That's a risk you have to take in order to get what you want."

Adele groaned, wondering why she had to become involved with this person or ghost or whatever she was.

"It's simple when you think about it," Jolene told her.

"And what does that mean?"

"You think I'm going to give you all this magic, all this power for nothing?" she asked. "Everything comes with a price." She paused for a moment then said with emphasis, "*Everything*."

That may have been true but Adele didn't know if she wanted to pay the price for it. But then she thought of little Cecelia being taken away and her heart twisted in pain at the memory. In fact, she knew she'd always feel pain over it. This was something she would never, ever get over. Therefore, she had to see her sister. She had to. And if that meant she had to what Jolene wanted, then that's what it meant.

"I'll do it," Adele said. "When do you want it done?"

"The sooner the better," Jolene said with a twinkle in her eye.

The Locket

About two weeks later, Jolene woke Adele at about midnight.

"It's time," she said.

Adele nodded and followed her to Head Mistress Tanner's office. There, Jolene pointed at a place on the wall.

"Push the wall," she said.

Adele stared at her, then pushed the wall. It popped open to reveal a closet. At the bottom of the closet was an old steel safe.

"Okay," Adele said. "Now what?"

"Open it," she said. "The combination is 38-33-90."

Adele didn't ask how she knew all this and then tried to open the safe. Of course, she couldn't crack it on the first try and had to give it a few more attempts before it finally popped open. Once it was open, she turned to Jolene and said, "Now what?"

"Now get me what I want," she said.

"And what is that?"

Jolene walked over, bent down and peered into the safe. Then she pointed. "There. I want that."

Adele looked in to see something at the very back of the safe. She grabbed it and pulled it out, then held it up. It was a gold locket in the shape of a heart. She stared at the heart, then at the engraving on the back which read, simply, "J."

"Open it," Jolene said.

Adele opened the heart to reveal a smiling, beautiful woman on one side and a smiling, handsome man on the other.

"Who are they?" Adele asked and looked at the smiling couple.

"My parents," she said and gave a soft smile. "They were always so good to me."

"Oh?"

She nodded, still smiling as she stared at them. "They never made me feel bad about myself. Not once."

"That's nice," Adele said, not knowing how to react to her words or her new mood.

Jolene stared at Adele and her smile deepened. "Yeah, they were great. They never hurt me, not once. Except for sending me here."

"What about that?"

She shrugged. "I didn't want to come."

"Why not?"

"Just didn't," she said.

Adele didn't press. She knew she wouldn't tell her anyway. She asked, "What are you going to do with it?"

"Put it on," Jolene said and nodded at her.

"But it's yours."

"No, it's yours now," she said. "Put it on."

Adele shrugged and put the locket around her neck. When she tried the clasp, she found that it was broken. She held it up to Jolene.

"Yeah, I forgot about that," she said. "Fix it."

"How?"

"You know how," Jolene said.

Adele sighed and held the locket in her hands then envisioned the clasp being repaired. She whispered, "*Mend, mend, mend...*" When she opened her hands, it was fixed. She put it on and turned to Jolene. "Why is this locket in the head mistresses' safe?"

"It just is," Jolene said and stood. She clapped her hands together and nodded vigorously.

Adele asked, "Now what?"

"Now we get you what you want."

Adele smiled. That's exactly what she wanted to hear.

"Tomorrow," Jolene said. "During class. Put a spell on your teacher and meet me in the bathroom."

Adele nodded.

"And wear the locket," Jolene said. "But hide it so no one sees."

"I will," Jolene said and shut the door to the safe. She stood and closed the door, then started out of the room. Before she left, Jolene held up one hand. "What is it?" Adele asked.

"I just want you to know that soon this will all be over," she told her.

"What does that mean?" Adele asked.

"It means, that soon this will all be over," she said, getting impatient. "Our work will be finished."

"And then what?" Adele asked.

"Then you're on your own," she said. "Do you think you will be able to handle it?"

Adele nodded. "I think so."

"Good," Jolene said. "Always have faith, Adele. Faith will see you through anything."

"I will try," Adele said. She turned to exit the room, then turned back around to say something else, but Jolene was gone. Adele sighed, then looked down at the locket and thought about Jolene's parents. The thought of why Jolene was haunting here at Bancroft House had crossed her mind fairly often. She wondered why Jolene wouldn't share how she got to be a ghost with her. She wanted to know what happened and why. But she knew it was pointless to ask, though she was certain this locket was a step in the direction of clarity on the issue.

The next day, Adele put a spell on her teacher. It was easy enough to do. She simply locked eyes with her and chanted to herself, *"I am excused. I am excused."*

"Yes, Adele," the teacher told her. "You are excused."

A few of the girls glanced at her, then at the teacher, wondering what that meant. Adele closed her eyes and said, *"Forget."*

Then the girls went back to their books as if nothing had happened. Adele smiled to herself and rose from her seat and slipped out of the room. Jolene was waiting on her in the bathroom, leaning against one of the sinks. When Adele entered, she jumped up and smiled at her.

"Finally," she said. "Let's do this." She held out her hands. Adele took them and waited. "Three times, three chants. Ready?"

Adele nodded.

"So, we begin," Jolene said and chanted, "'*Take me away, take me away, my sister is here, my sister is dear. Take me away, take me away, my sister is here, my sister is dear. Take me away, take me away, my sister is here, my sister is dear.*'"

"Got it," Adele said and then they both chanted, "*Take me away, take me away, my sister is here, my sister is dear. Take me away, take me away, my sister is here, my sister is dear. Take me away, take me away, my sister is here, my sister is dear.*"

Adele closed her eyes and felt that sense of weightlessness throughout her whole body. Then she felt herself lifting off the ground and then the ground beneath her feet disappeared. When she opened her eyes, she was sitting in front of a huge home. It looked like a French country house and sprawled out onto the immense lawn. It was pale yellow and the shrubbery was fancy and green.

"Wow," she said. "This is where Cecelia lives."

"It is," Jolene said. "Fancy, huh?"

Adele nodded. She could have never imagined living in a house like this. "I wonder where Cecelia is."

"Call her," Jolene said.

Adele nodded and closed her eyes. She called without saying a word, *"Cecelia, Cecelia, come to me. Come to me, Cecelia."*

Just then, Cecelia came out from the back of the house chasing a soccer ball. She giggled as it rolled across the yard. As soon as Adele saw her, her heart twisted in pain. She was so pretty and little. She was dressed in a pair of cute cut-off jean shorts and a pink t-shirt. Her feet were bare. She looked happy and content and so much healthier than she had at Bancroft House. Adele was glad, for a moment, she was really, really glad Cecelia had been adopted.

Adele walked over to her and stopped. Cecelia was about to pick up the ball when she saw her. She stood up straight and peered up at her. Adele was taken aback by her look. It was almost as if she wasn't too happy to see her. And that hurt her feelings.

"What are you doing here, Adele?" she asked.

"I came to check on you," she told her, bending down. "How are you?"

Cecelia looked around, then back at her. "Fine. Why are you here?"

"I just wanted to see you," she replied. "Are they good to you?"

"Yes."

"Really? Are they?"

"Yes," Cecelia said with impatience. "They are good to me. I love it here."

Adele waited for her to elaborate but she didn't. "Tell me more, Cecelia."

She sighed with the impatience of a seven-year-old and shook her head. "More what? Listen, I have to get back. We're playing soccer ball."

"But I'm here to see you," Adele said, feeling a flash of anger. "I went through a lot of trouble to get here."

Cecelia shrugged. "I'm sorry. I just have to get back."

"Fine," Adele said. "Just tell me a little about living here. Do you have to sleep in the attic or anything?"

"No," Cecelia said, almost rolling her eyes. "It's not like that here. I have my own room. I have dolls and clothes and all the good food I want to eat and not just candy. I eat roast beef and asparagus and stuff like that."

Adele didn't know if she wanted to hear all of this.

"I was hurt that they took me, at first," she continued. "I was mad that they didn't take you and Eliza, too, but they explained that they couldn't. I'm sorry, but I like it here. I like my new parents."

Adele turned away.

"Adele," she said, laying a hand on her shoulder. "They love me."

"How do you know?" she asked, not looking at her.

"They tell me they do."

Adele stiffened and wanted to move away from Cecelia. It was the first time she didn't want to be around her. She'd never felt anything like this but her emotions were in such a torrent, she felt overwhelmed. But she knew it was true. She knew these people loved her sister. She'd observed enough to know that they were good to her.

"I wish you and Eliza could be here with me." Cecelia paused and took her hand away. "But... But..."

"But we can't," Adele finished for her. She turned to her and a dark anger rose up in her when she stared into her little sister's beautiful gray-blue eyes.

Adele didn't know why she was feeling the way she was and she couldn't figure out why knowing her sister had it so good made her angry, but it did. She wanted to feel better knowing she was well taken care of but knowing what she and Eliza went through each and every day made her resent it. Why couldn't someone want them, too? Why did they only want her? Of course, Cecelia was younger and that meant she was cuter and more precious. She needed someone to take good care of her. She and Eliza could make it, albeit, barely, where they were. But the school would have eventually broken Cecelia and she knew that. But she still had a hard time overcoming the jealousy that something really great had happened for her and not for herself and her other sister.

Just then, Cecelia's eyes welled up with tears and Adele understood how badly Cecelia needed this, how badly she needed a family. Adele also wanted a family and within this family, she wanted her sisters. She wanted them to be wanted as a whole, not torn apart and picked over. And little Cecelia needed this more than she or even Eliza. She was more sensitive, more delicate than they were. She was the baby and had always been treated as such.

"I wish you and Eliza could live with me," Cecelia said as the tears poured down her cheeks. "But you can't. And you can't take this away from me, Adele! I can't go back there. My hands bleed everyday! Please don't ruin this for me. I don't want to go back there."

Adele started crying, too. She understood the hardship they were put through and for someone to do it to such a small child was just wrong. She threw her arms around her little sister and hugged her tight. She vowed to never let her go; even though she knew the only place she'd be near was in her heart. She would never again think harshly of her sister. She would never again resent her for her good fortune. And she would never again visit her until she had the money to take her back. She promised herself all of this that day and she planned to keep her promise.

"Shh," Adele whispered and wiped the tears from her face. "I would never do anything to hurt you, little sister. You know that."

Cecelia nodded and smiled at her. "I know that. I just want you to know that they're good to me and maybe one day I can talk them into letting you and Eliza come and stay. I've talked to them before. They said maybe."

Adele shook her head. "Don't ask them again. When they're ready, they'll tell you. Don't be a bother, just be a good daughter and they will love you like their own."

Cecelia smiled widely. "They already do."

Adele didn't doubt it for a moment. How could anyone not love Cecelia, as little and as special and as cute as she was? She had something most people could not resist.

Just then, a young woman came around the house, looking around frantically. "Cecelia!" she hollered and stopped when she saw them.

"Who's that?" Adele asked.

"My nanny," Cecelia said. "I have one and Mabel has one, too. I like her. She's nice."

Adele's mouth almost dropped to the ground. But then she forced a smile and nodded at her. "Give me a quick hug then go back to playing."

She bent down and hugged her tightly then she let her go. Cecelia waved at her as she hurried to her nanny. Adele watched her and just as the nanny started to question her presence, she threw her hand up at her and said, *"Forget."*

The nanny's head jerked a little, then she focused on Cecelia, smiling at her. "I wondered where you'd gotten off to. Come on!"

Cecelia grabbed the nanny's hand and took one last look at Adele and then disappeared around the back of the house. Adele watched her go and felt a great sense of loss. She knew she'd never have Cecelia back again. But it didn't bother her as much as she thought it would. The main reason being that she knew she was very well taken care of. The kid had it good now and Adele didn't want to hamper that in any way.

"Let's go," Jolene said, walking up to her.

"Alright," Adele replied and turned to her.

"It's for the best," Jolene said.

"That's easy for you to say."

Jolene rolled her eyes. "You have to learn to let go, Adele. If you don't, you'll never be a powerful witch."

"Who says I want to?" Adele said.

"Well, it's better than the alternative," Jolene said. "Seriously, though, let go and you will find that your life gets easier."

"I do let go," Adele snapped. "It's just that she's gone now and it's killing me."

"Just let it go."

"But what about me? What about Eliza? What about us being without our little sister?"

"Let it go," Jolene said. "You need to learn to let go."

"I do let go," Adele said again. "Why do you keep saying that? I do let go."

"No, you really don't."

"Yes, I do," she said, ready to start crying again, this time out of frustration.

"No, you don't."

"How so?"

"Like with commanding things," she said. "Like with the book the night we met. That's one of the hardest things to do. And it's hard because most people can't get past how easy it is. They can't relax their minds and just allow things to happen. They always question everything. You have to learn when to stop questioning and when to just receive. When a person is unsure of themselves, they start to beg rather than ask. Don't beg, ever."

"I don't," Adele said, staring at her. "Besides, you told me it was one of the easiest things to do, commanding the book to come to me."

"No, it's one of the hardest."

"But why did you tell me that?"

"If I told you how hard it was, you'd never been able to do it," she said and shook her head in annoyance. "But I knew if you could do it on your own, I could teach you anything. It's about having an open mind and being willing to learn, Adele."

"Oh, really?"

She nodded. "The trick is to allow it to happen, Adele. Remember—no forcing. And if you can get past that roadblock, you have it. Magic is yours for the taking. Most people can't get past that because they want to put too much into it; they want to analyze it to death. You don't have to do that with magic. You just have to be and allow the magic to be what it is."

"Oh, that makes sense," Adele said and refrained from rolling her eyes. "But I don't care. Not right now. I just don't care."

Jolene stared at her and sighed. "Come on," she said, holding out her hands. "This will probably drain me for a week, but you need it. Come on."

"What are you doing?"

"You mean, what am I doing for you," she said. "Come on. Climb aboard."

Adele didn't really want to. She wanted to wallow in her misery a little longer. But what was the use in that? She grabbed onto Jolene's hands.

"Three chants," she said. "*Take me away, home sweet home, take me away, to where I belong, home sweet home.*"

And so they chanted, three times, "*Take me away, home sweet home, take me away, to where I belong, home sweet home. Take me away, home sweet home, take me away, to where I belong, home sweet home. Take me away, home sweet home, take me away, to where I belong, home sweet home.*"

Adele squeezed her eyes shut and felt her body lift off the ground. Then, all of a sudden, they fell onto a beach. When she opened her eyes, she had to squint because the sun was so bright. It was warm and the ocean spread out vastly in front of them. Adele turned to see lots of people milling about. Some were sunbathing, some were enjoying the water and some were just walking, splashing their feet in the surf. She stared at the pier for a moment before turning to Jolene who was standing, dusting sand off her skirt.

"What is this place?"

"Cocoa Beach," she said.

"Florida?" Adele asked, looking around. "Like in *I Dream of Jeannie?*"

Jolene almost doubled over with laughter. "Yeah! I would have never made that connection. But, of course, you would have."

"Oh," Adele said. "I just always loved that show."

Jolene stopped laughing and pointed down the beach towards and an older looking motel. It was one-level and nice but just a little rundown. However, something about it seemed really cool. It might have been the thatch roof or the tiki bar or even the surfboards that were lined up in front of it, along with wetsuits hanging on the railing of the steps that lead down to the beach. It seemed laid back and hip, like it didn't care what anyone thought of it.

"A beach house can never be too shabby," Jolene said, as if reading her thoughts. "That's what gives it its charm. And that goes double for an old beach motel."

"Okay," Adele said, not sure of what she was agreeing to.

"It's my father's motel," she said.

"Oh, wow," Adele replied. "Does he know? I mean, does he know about you being a ghost?"

"No," she said. "If he knew I was ghost, he'd try to séance me."

"What does that mean?"

"He'd try to find me and bring me to him," she said. "For answers."

"Answers about what?"

"My death," she said. "And I'm not ready for that."

"Your death?" Adele asked.

"Did you never pause for one second and ask yourself how I became a ghost?"

"I did," Adele said, "I mean, I have. But then it was just too creepy, so I pushed it out of my mind."

Jolene laughed. "Good girl. Anyway, that's his motel; he runs it. He lives there with his new wife and their new kid. I have a brother. His name is Max."

"Do you come here a lot?"

She shook her head. "No, not a lot. A few times a year just to check up on things and visit Max. He knows about me. I've been visiting him for a while… Well, since he was a baby. He's never been scared of me and he knows to keep it quiet."

"Oh, really?" Adele asked.

"He's a big boy now," she said. "In fact, he's a few years older than you."

"I thought he was a baby," Adele said.

"He was, just like you were once and just like me," she said, smiling softly. "Once."

Adele nodded. "Now what?"

"What do you mean?"

"Why are we here?" Adele asked.

Jolene smiled at her then turned to the ocean. "That's why we're here. Turn around and look at it."

Adele turned around and stared at the vast ocean and was in awe. She'd never seen the ocean before. It was wide, watery and beautiful. It had a calming effect on her. She sat down in the sand and sighed. Where was she going to go now? What was she going to do? And why had Jolene brought her here?

Jolene sat down next to her and laid a hand on her shoulder for a moment before removing it. They didn't speak, only watched the water crash into the sand. Adele looked out to see surfers sitting on their boards, lopping up and down in the waves. They were talking to each other and laughing.

"I didn't know they surfed here," Adele said.

"Yeah, some of the best surfers in the world come from around here, and Melbourne, too." Jolene paused and smiled. "The waves swell really good over there near the pier," she continued and pointed. "Oh, there's Max. He loves to surf."

Adele squinted to get a better look but couldn't make heads or tails out about him.

"Don't you just love it here?" Jolene asked.

"I do," Adele said. "I wish I could live here."

"Maybe one day you will," Jolene said. "But not today. We have to get back."

Adele nodded and turned to her. "Thank you. I feel better even though I do blame you for Cecelia."

Jolene shook her head. "It was an inevitability, Adele. Sooner or later one of you would have been adopted out. That's just the way it goes. I just made sure she hit the jackpot."

"I just want her to be okay," Adele said quietly.

"She will be better than okay," Jolene said. "And so will you and Eliza. Soon enough you will see that."

Adele stared at her, wondering what she meant. But Jolene was staring out at Max and grinning. Just then, he caught a big wave and began to ride it out. Jolene grinned and raised her arms, shouting, "*Bigger, bigger, bigger!*"

The wave got bigger and bigger and bigger. Max was ecstatic as any surfer would be.

"*Hold*," Jolene said. "*Hold!*"

Max held on and rode the wave out. Adele noticed everyone on the beach was watching him and the wave with rapt attention. It was mesmerizing and she wondered for a moment if he might fall off and hurt himself. But he didn't. No matter how the wave swelled, he hung on, almost as if he were conquering it. Within seconds, it was over and he rode the wave all the way to the shore where he stepped off his board like a pro.

All the people on the beach started clapping. He grinned good-naturedly and accepted pats on the back and hooted and hollered a little himself. It was quite a scene. Adele was mesmerized by it, by the camaraderie between

Max and the other surfers and everyone else on the beach. It almost bordered on a higher ground, akin to spirituality.

Adele stepped back and watched it all. Then she studied Max. He looked a lot like Jolene, with blonde hair and blue eyes. His hair was shaggy and kept falling into his eyes and his body was long and lean, that of a surfers. He was very attractive but Adele couldn't get over how much he and Jolene looked alike. It was almost creepy.

Once the hoopla died down, Max looked around, smiling, then whispered loud enough for Adele to hear, "I know you're here, sis. Thanks."

Jolene grinned. "That's my little bro. Hang-ten, baby, hang-ten!"

Adele started to say something but Jolene shook her head.

"We have to go now, Adele," she said and grabbed her hands. "But did you see it? Did you see it?"

"What?"

"Magic," she said. "Did you see the joy it brought to him? To everyone else?"

Adele nodded.

"And that's why you can never turn your back on it," Jolene said. "You have to ride it out, just like Max rode that wave out."

"I will," Adele said.

"Good," Jolene said. "Let's go back now."

And so they did, leaving the sunshine and the beach for Bancroft House. Once they returned, it was as if the clock had been turned back. Adele went back to her class, no one took notice and then she finished out her day, wondering exactly how magic was going to play out in her life.

The Spring Formal

Every year, the rich girls of Bancroft House held a spring formal where they would invite boys from the other private schools in the area to attend. It was like a prom, only the girls and boys didn't attend as couples. They only got together once the dance began. It was a big deal to the rich girls because this was one day of the year where they could get dressed up, sip punch and flirt with boys. They might even be able to steal a kiss or two in a darkened corner of the house.

The rich girls were all aflutter with the impending festivities and giggled to themselves for weeks before the actual event took place. Adele mostly ignored them and couldn't wait for it to be over. She was sick of seeing the posters "Spring Formal!" throughout the downstairs halls and listening to the chatter about the event. But, of course, she soon found out that she would have to work the formal.

"Oh, please," she groaned to Ms. Ingles. "Do I have to?"

"Why, Adele," she snapped. "I thought you'd be pleased."

"But they don't like me," Adele said. "I shouldn't be near any of them."

"Know your place. You're a good server and so you will serve," she said and turned and left the kitchen.

Adele watched her go then groaned. Great! Now, in addition to everything else she had to put up with, she had to serve punch at this stupid dance. She just knew the rich girl she'd slapped would be there smirking, saying mean things to her. She began to feel overly anxious about it and almost wanted to run away.

"What are you looking so pensive about?" Jolene asked out of nowhere.

Adele jerked and looked around. Jolene was sitting across from her at the little table. She raised an eyebrow. Adele shrugged and sat back. "Nothing."

"Okay, whatever," Jolene said. "What are you going to do this summer?"

"What do you mean?"

"When the school closes."

Adele stared at her. "I don't know."

"School will be out before you know it," she said. "They usually let all the other girls stay during the summer but I have heard there are summer work programs, at camps and things. You should look into that."

Great," Adele replied. "More work."

"It would be better than staying here, wouldn't it?" she asked. "I bet Eliza would like to get out for the summer too."

Adele nodded. "I'll check into it."

"You should," she said and started grinning. "So, you're going to the spring formal?"

Adele looked at her and couldn't help but grin back. Jolene was such a smart-aleck. "So, you know?"

"I know everything," Jolene said. "What's the big deal?"

"I hate the rich girls," Adele said.

"No, you don't," she said. "You just want them to like you and they won't because they're raised to look down on poor girls like yourself."

"It's hardly that," Adele said. "They just make me feel bad about myself."

"Inferiority is an inferior emotion," Jolene said smugly.

"I suppose it is," Adele said and picked at her food. She stopped and looked at Jolene. "Did you go to the spring formal when you were here?"

"No," she said. "I didn't feel like it."

"What do you mean?"

She shrugged. "I'd gotten my heart broken, that's what I mean. And, after that, I didn't care. And, after that, I died, so it was pointless. Love, I mean."

Adele was almost disturbed at her nonchalance but she let it go. Jolene could be really macabre at times. But, then again, she was a ghost.

"But *you* shouldn't give up on love," Jolene said.

"I think I kind of have to," she replied. "So, who was the boy? The one who broke your heart?"

"No one special," she replied and looked away. "Oh, there's the hall monitor."

Adele looked over to see Lotta hurrying towards her and chuckled. Jolene didn't like Lotta much and would always call her the hall monitor because it seemed as though Lotta popped up a lot around them when they least expected it and interrupted their work. And she'd always tell Adele it was time to "get back to class" or "get back to work" or "get to bed" or whatever. It really got on Adele's nerves, too. She *was* like a hall monitor.

"We have to go and set up the ballroom now," Lotta said. "Come on."

"Why are we so rushed?" Adele asked. "The formal isn't until Friday."

"That's just what they told me," she replied.

Adele nodded and rose from her seat. She glanced back at Jolene who was watching them.

"Go on," Jolene said. "I'll see you later."

Adele nodded and followed Lotta out of the kitchen and all the way to the gigantic ballroom. They paused at the door and Lotta turned to her, giving her a peculiar look.

"What is it?" Adele asked.

Lotta leaned forward and stared at the locket around her neck. "Where did you get that?"

"Oh," Adele said and pushed it back under her shirt, trying to come up with an explanation that didn't involve Jolene. "It was my mom's," she finally said.

Lotta nodded but didn't say anything else as they entered the ballroom. Inside, there was a hubbub of activity and about ten other girls were setting up seating along one of the walls and others were arranging tables for the punch and finger foods. Still others were hanging streamers from the ceiling. All Adele could think of was all the work it was going to take for them to give the rich girls a good time and then all the work afterwards when they had to take it all down. Work, work, and more work. Adele thought that's all her life was. The thought made her feel overwhelmed and tired.

"Come on," Lotta said. "You can help get the linens out of the back room."

Adele nodded then stopped her from walking off. "Hey, what are you going to do this summer?"

"What do you mean?"

"I mean," she said. "Are you going to stay around here or go for a work program?"

Lotta's eyes nearly popped out of her head. "Work program? I didn't know anything about that."

Adele nodded. "Yeah, I heard there are work programs at camps and stuff."

"Where did you hear this?"

Adele clamped her mouth shut. "Umm… I don't know. I just assumed—"

Lotta cut her off, "Adele, you have to stay here. There aren't any work programs."

"I think there are," she said and looked over Lotta's shoulder to see Jane approaching them.

"Are what?" Jane asked, walking up.

"Work programs," Adele said.

Jane laughed. "Yeah, we're in one. Didn't you know that the summer is one of the busiest times for the flower factory?"

Adele was taken aback. Why had Jolene mentioned this? She suddenly felt a pinch on her arm. She jerked it back and saw Jolene standing there, fuming at her.

"That was for your ears only," she hissed. "You don't tell these idiots anything I say! Now they'll go blabber it all over the place."

Adele didn't respond. She looked at Lotta and said, "Sorry, I just thought we could get out of here for the summer."

"There is no getting out," Jane said and walked off. "Not until you're eighteen."

Jolene watched her go and shook her head. "I just can't stand that girl."

Adele glanced at her then turned to leave. It was going to be a long night. Again.

The formal was in full swing by eight that Saturday night. All the rich girls had their finest party dresses on and were interacting with the good looking boys from the area's private schools. There were tall boys and short boys and thin boys and muscular boys. They all looked good and the rich girls were beside themselves with school girl crushes. They were all keyed up with giggles and batting eyes. Adele watched them, thinking about how foolish they were acting. But then again, it might have been bitterness talking.

She stood at her station behind the big punch bowl, and watched with as much dispassion as she could muster. She didn't know how she was going to be able to stand doing this.

She looked around and her eyes settled on a boy who was standing by himself at the back of the room. He leaned against the wall with confidence, as if he were just waiting for someone. He must have felt her staring at him because he suddenly glanced up and locked eyes with her for a couple of seconds. Adele blushed and looked down quickly. When she looked back up, he was grinning at her.

Adele couldn't take her eyes off of him. The boy—tall, dark and handsome—sent the pangs of first love into her heart and made it swell. She'd never felt this way about a boy before. And she'd just only noticed him! But he'd noticed her, too, and he couldn't seem to take his eyes off of her.

"You'll never have him," Jolene whispered in her ear.

Adele ignored her for as long as she could. Jolene observed this and sat down in a chair behind her with a sigh.

"Give it up," she told her.

"Shut up," Adele replied, refusing to look at her.

"He is cute, though," she said. "Oh, look at you! You're blushing."

Just then, a young boy whose face was covered with acne came up and asked for a glass of punch. Adele served him and he mumbled his thanks and walked away.

"Now that one likes you," Jolene said giggling. "I can tell it!"

"Shut up!" Adele hissed. "And go away."

"No, this is fun," she said. "I do so love these spring formals!"

Adele looked back over at the boy. He was still standing there, still waiting on someone. He was still watching her. She blushed again and couldn't believe how she was acting. She was going all ga-ga over this young man and she didn't even know him! She was acting worse than all the rich girls combined. And she didn't even have a shot with him, none at all. She sighed and sat down in the chair next to Jolene's.

"Oh, he'd see around your poverty," Jolene said. "For a while. But then you wouldn't mesh with his family and his mom would hate you. And then... Ooh! Oh, yes! And then the jealous ex-girlfriend will put a spell on you for taking her man!"

Adele looked up to see the rich girl she'd slapped enter, lock her eyes on the boy and then put her arms around his neck.

"You got to be kidding me," Adele said, thinking how unfair life could be sometimes. Why her? *Why?*

"Sucks to be you," Jolene said. "Who would have thought?"

"I'm surprised you didn't set this up," Adele told her.

"Me? I never interfere in the game of love."

"Yeah, right," Adele said. "I wonder what his name is."

"Declan," she said. "That's an Irish name. Or maybe English. Maybe it's Irish? It doesn't matter."

"How do you know this?" Adele asked.

"It's on his nametag," she said. "In case you haven't noticed, everyone except you is wearing one."

That was true. Adele had forgotten to put one on. And she certainly wasn't going to do it now. She wished she didn't even have to be there. She stared at the rich girl who was basically throwing herself at Declan and got an idea.

"I'm going to take him away from her," Adele said out of nowhere, surprising herself.

"Why?" Jolene asked.

"Huh?"

"I mean, why bother? It doesn't seem like much of a challenge."

"It's not for him," Adele said. "Though he is cute. It's because I want to see if I can have him. You know, to see if I can take him away from her."

"Ooh, listen to you!" she exclaimed and laughed. "I love it! You're like a minx or something. What do you have against her anyway?"

Adele shrugged, not wanting to get into it.

"Oh, because she tripped you and you slapped her and then all that…"

"How do you know that?" Adele asked.

"I'm a ghost," Jolene said. "I'm nosy."

Adele just stared at her.

"Do you think all I do all day is hang around waiting to talk to you?" she asked and scoffed. "No, I have to haunt. It's part of my job. And I love scaring the bejesus out of the rich girls. They're so dainty!"

Adele couldn't help but laugh. "What do you do to them?"

"I generally just creep them out. I also 'misplace' their things, like toothbrushes or jewelry, stuff like that," she said. "And then they get all in an uproar and start accusing each other of doing stuff. It's so funny. And I also stand behind them when they're looking in the mirror and then they see me and jerk around and get all scared. I *love* doing that."

Adele smiled at her. "What about her? Ever do anything to her?"

"*Her* name is Jewel," Jolene said. "And she is about to graduate. She's been here, just so you'll know, since she was twelve, even longer than you."

"I don't care about her name," Adele said. "But have you ever done anything to her?"

Jolene shrugged. "Not really. I scared her in the hall a few times, that's about it. She's very skittish. Now she won't walk anywhere alone." She chuckled and stared at Adele. "Keep in mind that taking him from her is no challenge. I wouldn't even bother."

"She embarrassed me and got me banished from the dining room!"

"And you eat better as a result," Jolene said. "And you got to meet a ghost who's given you some really cool power. What has she done? Brushed her hair a hundred times a night? Pined for good looking Declan? Wow. What a life!"

Adele noted her sarcasm but she still didn't like the girl, Jewel. Just then, another boy came up wanting punch. Adele didn't feel like dealing with him, so she whispered, "*Go away*," and he did. Yeah, having magical powers was sometimes convenient. She couldn't argue with that.

"Maybe I won't try," Adele said. "What's the point?"

"Smart girl," Jolene said.

Just then Adele glanced up to see Jewel staring at her. As soon as she noticed Adele staring back, she smirked at her. It was like she was challenging her.

"No, no," Adele said. "I am going to do it."

"What?" Jolene asked and stared at her.

"She thinks she is so much better than me," Adele said. "It's not fair. I am going to do it."

"As your friend and as your magic teacher, I think this is a bad idea," Jolene said. "Let it go."

"I won't," Adele said. "I have magic on my side, don't I?"

Jolene stared at her then sighed. "I suppose you do."

"You with me or not?"

Jolene leaned back and said, "Tell me what you have in mind."

Adele thought about it for a few minutes then turned to Jolene and said, "I have to become of them. I have to become a rich girl, if only for tonight."

"I think I'm going to like where you're going with this," Jolene told her.

She grinned at Jolene and got up and left the room. She went into the bathroom that was down the hall and, after locking herself in a stall, she sat down and closed her eyes. Then she imagined herself wearing a beautiful party dress. She waited for about two minutes before opening her eyes. She gasped in delight when she looked up to see the garment hanging on the back of the door. It was a deep blue princess cut gown, which would come to just above her ankles. The skirt flowed out and had a lighter colored blue tulle overlaying the satin. The tulle was covered here and there with sparkly rhinestones. It was the most beautiful dress she'd ever seen.

Adele giggled and hurriedly dressed, taking off her drab uniform and slipping the gown over her head. It fit like a glove. But there was something missing. Shoes! She had forgotten the shoes! She closed her eyes and imagined a pair of sparkly, silver stilettos, ones that would be a perfect match to the dress. When she opened her eyes, they were on the floor next to her feet. They were about four inches high and the size of them almost intimidated her. But they were gorgeous! But what if she fell? What if she twisted her ankle? Oh, what did it matter? They were so cool! She pushed her feet into the shoes and found that she could stand very easily in them.

When she came out of the stall, Jolene was sitting on one of the sinks. She studied her and nodded with approval.

"You look stunning," she told her. "Seriously good. But you need to fix your hair."

Jolene looked in the mirror and envisioned a fabulous style. She closed her eyes and when she reopened them, half of her hair was pulled back with a silver barrette and the other half was curled and falling beautifully around her shoulders.

"Cute," Jolene said. "Now for your makeup."

Adele closed her eyes and imagined her face done up with glamorous makeup. When she reopened them, the makeup was perfect and she looked a little older but really gorgeous. She couldn't help but smile at herself. She looked so good. And she actually looked happy, which did make a difference. She felt the soft murmur of excitement began to build inside of her. She was actually going to talk to a boy! She was actually going to the formal! She couldn't believe it. She was going to go through with it.

"A little like Sophia Loren," Jolene said. "Love it!"

"It does look good," Adele said.

"Now, make sure that everyone knows you're one of them," she said. "You're a rich girl tonight, just like Cinderella was. Right?"

Adele nodded. She knew what to do. She had to act like a rich girl in order to talk to Declan.

"And be done by midnight."

"Why?" Adele asked. "Will the dress turn back into my rags?"

Jolene laughed. "No! God, where do you come up with this stuff? I mean, you don't need to push your luck is all. Go out there, have a good time and I'll see you later. Oh, and put the dress back up here. Someone will think someone forgot it. You don't want to have to explain where it came from."

Adele nodded. "You're right."

Jolene hopped up and came over to her and smiled. "It's like I'm sending my little girl to prom. I'd hug you if I could!"

"I thought you could hug me," Adele said.

"I mean if I wanted to."

Adele stared at her. Jolene burst out laughing.

"You fall for it every time!" Jolene said. "Such an inferiority complex! Here!" She gave her a quick hug and then pulled back.

Adele laughed then stopped. "Oh, my God, what if I mess up and get caught? What if I can't remember the magic to pull this off?"

"You and your nerves!" Jolene half-shouted. "Just go with it. Go with the flow. Let go and allow the magic to happen. Can you do that?"

"I can," Adele said.

"Then go and have a good time."

She smiled and then left the bathroom, walking carefully in the high heels. When she reached the ballroom, she closed her eyes, took a deep breath and focused on all the people in there. She chanted, "*I am one of you; I am one of you*," several times and then sent that thought off and then she imagined herself being one of them, being a rich girl, being accepted. She imagined everyone knowing who she was and she was a rich girl at the spring formal.

"*I am one of you*," she whispered and opened the door. The formal was now in full swing. No one stopped dancing or even really paid attention to her as she entered. She glanced at the other girls, especially Lotta and Jane, but they didn't take notice of her and continued their tasks.

She smiled to herself and looked around the crowd for Declan. She finally found him dancing with Jewel, like he didn't want to be there. Jewel was all over him and was really making a fool out of herself. Adele made a note to never make a fool out of herself over a boy. Adele could tell Jewel really liked, if not loved, this boy. The realization almost made her back off. But why should she? If he didn't love her, why shouldn't he have the option to see someone else? Adele knew there was a spark between her and him, even if she was just another other girl, even if she had to pretend to be a rich girl to get to him. She wanted to know what that spark was all about and to see what if felt like to be liked, really, really liked by a boy. That's what propelled her to do this, not getting back at Jewel for being so mean. It was about feeling wanted by someone else. *How would that feel?*

She was surprised that she didn't even have to do anything to get him to notice her. He looked up, spotted her and grinned. She couldn't help but smile back and then thought she didn't want to meet him like this. Suddenly, her nerves got the best of her and she just wanted to run and hide. So, she turned and left the room. No one saw her, no one noticed. She hurried out and then down the hall and out onto the veranda. She took a moment to catch her breath and realized that she shouldn't have done this. She shouldn't have tried to take Declan away from Jewel. She was playing too much with other's emotions and that always had the potential to backfire.

Adele made up her mind to go back to the bathroom and change back into her old clothes and to forget about this. She was about to do just that when she turned and saw Declan standing there. He had come after her. That meant... That meant he liked her. And then everything made sense. She couldn't help but smile. He grinned back but hesitated to make a move, as if he were unsure of how to proceed. So, she took the reins.

"Hello," she said.

"Hi," he replied. "I thought... I don't know. I mean, who are you?"

She held out her hand. "I'm Adele."

"Declan," he said and shook her hand, then held it for a moment longer than he should have. "Have we met?"

Had they? Adele's mind began to calculate the formula of the magic she'd just produced. Had she forgotten something? Left something out? Or was it him with the problem? Oh, no, what if he hadn't been looking at her? Had she done something wrong?

"I mean, I know I saw you earlier, in the ballroom," he said, explaining. "But I feel like I know you from somewhere else, too."

"Oh," Adele said and breathed a sigh of relief. The spell was fine. "No, we haven't met before."

"Oh," he said and couldn't take his eyes off her. "You look beautiful."

"Thanks," she replied and gave him a small smile.

"You are stunning," he said. "Hey, I know! Let's do something. What do you want to do?"

She grinned. "I don't know. What do you want to do?"

He shrugged. "Let's ditch."

She couldn't stop smiling. "Okay. Where to?"

"My house," he said.

Adele stopped for a second and common sense came back to her. What if he was up to something?

"Or not," he said. "My family owns a lake house not too far from here. I just hate these things."

"What about Jewel?" she asked.

"What about her?" he replied.

She smiled again and felt that she could trust him, though her guard was going to be up. But then she felt weird. She'd never been alone with a boy before. She didn't know if she'd even know how to act. But something told her to just stop, to just wait a minute, to just see. She didn't know what to do.

Then it occurred to her. There was no future with this boy. She was not only wasting her time but his as well. Even magic couldn't take away that fact. They were worlds apart and the realization hit her like a ton of bricks. If she proceeded with him, he'd have to know everything about her and then what? What if he betrayed her? She knew he was a good soul; she could tell that. But even good souls can sometimes get hurt and out of hurt they can lash out in fear and anger. And that's when the trouble should start.

It's a choice, she thought to herself. *I'm a witch now. I have responsibility.* And she felt it, felt being a witch. And witches couldn't be like every other young girl. Witches had to protect themselves and their craft. They couldn't go around flaunting themselves and they couldn't allow just anyone into their lives. It was a choice, a hard choice but Adele knew she had to make it. This young man, as beautiful and as sincere as he was, was not her future. He was not even a distraction. There was no future with him and any distraction he could provide would probably not be to her betterment.

So why torture herself with it? She could see herself lying awake at night pining over him. She could feel the heartache that loving someone like him would bring and the misery. And hadn't she already been miserable enough?

"Come on," he said. "Let's go have some fun."

She noticed that there was a bit of desperation in his voice. He really wanted to be with her. He really liked her. But she knew it wasn't meant to be. She knew this wasn't the route to take and she'd proved her point. She had taken him away from the rich girl, Jewel. She stared at him, staring at her and her heart twisted in pain. But she knew this wasn't her destiny. This was just a diversion. This was something that could end badly and bring more pain. She'd had enough pain. She wanted some joy.

"Adele?" he asked.

"Shh," she said and stepped up to him, pressing her finger against his lips. Then she smiled, tiptoed and brushed her lips across his. This made him draw in his breath softly and make a grab for her. She smiled and pulled back.

"Go inside and forget," she said.

"No," he said. "Don't do this to me."

She shook her head. "No, go inside and forget. *Forget.*"

He stared at her then her command took effect. He turned and walked away from her and left her for Jewel, a rich girl, someone more like himself. She watched him go and felt a sadness well up inside of her that was almost unbearable. The tears pooled in her eyes and fell onto her cheeks but she knew she had made the right decision. Her life and his were just too different. She understood that now. Now she understood what it meant to be a witch. But where all this would lead her was still completely and totally unknown.

"You did the right thing," Jolene said.

"Did I?" Adele asked without looking at her. She was still staring at the place he'd been standing, almost wishing she could take it all back.

"You did," she said. "You'd only break his heart."

Adele turned to her and threw her a sharp look. "Break *his* heart?"

She nodded. "Boys like that fall hard for girls like us. And they never understand us, either. They don't get it, the magic. All they can see is how it takes us away from them."

Adele stared at her and wondered what she was getting at. She wanted to ask how she knew all this, how she understood so much, but she kept quiet.

"You will understand, too, with time," Jolene said and if reading her thoughts. "When you get older, you will know what it means to let go and it will stop bothering you."

"Is this why you didn't want me to do it?" Adele asked.

"Yes, it is," Jolene said. "But it's an important lesson to learn, Adele. We're different. It's hard to mesh with other people who don't share our craft."

Adele didn't answer. She looked down at her dress and sighed. She was just a poor girl dressed up like Cinderella. But, unlike Cinderella, Adele would not be returning to any castle to claim her throne. Adele was just a poor girl dressed in rich girl's clothes. That's all she was. But she knew now that she could be so much more. Where she had been would cease to matter; what was important was where she was going. But where that was could have been anyone's guess.

The Bad Man

Adele got through the spring formal and everything went back to normal for a while. She slipped back into her work routine and dreamed about leaving Bancroft House. She kept a close eye on Eliza, too, and hoped that something would work out where they could leave the place together. Eliza was getting taller. She was making that slow transition from cute little girl into beautiful young woman. She was going to be thirteen soon and she needed more than this house could give her. However, that was pretty much out of her hands until she turned eighteen.

But spring was almost over and soon it would be summer. Adele was still unsure what she was going to do. She was interested in doing a summer work program but Jolene had told her not to talk to anyone about it. She kept her mouth shut and wondered how this was going to play out.

Additionally, she was almost all the way through *The Big Book of Magic for Girls*. She was learning new spells everyday and her power as a witch was growing. She could feel it. It was like she was always tingling, always on the verge of a new discovery. And she was. Every day as she grew stronger, she came into her own more and more. Jolene liked her progress but told her not to let it go to her head and to always study and to always practice. And, she warned, to never, ever let anyone know what she was. This was a secret she didn't have a hard time keeping.

Nevertheless, secrets sometimes have a way of coming out even when a person holds them as close to their hearts as they can. Sometimes, secrets become known and when that happens, there is usually a price to pay. Adele didn't realize it at the time, but she was soon going to be found out for what she was.

It happened during dinner. It was late April. Adele was in her usual seat in the kitchen and had just finished eating when she heard a commotion going on in the dining room. As soon as she heard it, all of her senses became alert. She had never felt that way before and it almost spooked her. But something told her to get up and go see what was happening.

She glanced over at the cooks, who were staring at each other in confusion. One was still stirring the soup in the pot. Another one was washing dishes and the other one had stopped mid-step in the middle of the kitchen holding a loaf of fresh-baked bread. Adele stared at them, thinking of how they resembled a still-life painting, then turned her attention to the dining room. She had to get in there.

She got up, walked over to the swinging door and pushed it open. The whole place was in chaos. Girls were screaming. Some were cowering. Some were trying to leave. And in the middle of all this was a man, a crazy, wild-looking man. He was probably in his late thirties and he looked deranged. He was on a rampage. He was destroying things, throwing chairs across the room and turning over tables. Plates of food were flying through the air. He was scaring all the girls so badly they were shaking, and looking for the exit, which he'd blocked with a few tables. Adele watched as he threw a heavy crystal vase across the room, barely missing the tops of several girls' heads. It dented the wall and then fell to the floor and smashed into pieces.

Who was this man? And why was he doing this? Adele had to gain her bearings before she could make any sense of it. *Where did he come from?*

He turned on the room, bent at the waist like a gorilla and roared. He looked almost ridiculous. But he was dangerous, as any mad man might have been. Then, out of nowhere, he charged a small group of girls who were in the corner. Adele saw that Eliza was in the group. Fear rose up in her so strong that she knew she would have to do something about him.

"Stop!" she screamed without thinking, without thought. *"Stop!"*

The man suddenly stopped in his tracks, frozen. He didn't even turn to her. He just stood there like he'd been rendered immobile. And he had. But then Adele realized something. Everyone else in the room was frozen too, but not like him, not like the bad man. They were all frozen because they were all stunned and they were all looking at her. All eyes in the room had turned to her. Then it was her time to freeze. *Oh, no, what have I done?* The thought came at her so swiftly she almost fell to her feet. She searched the room for Eliza. She found her and their eyes met. And then Eliza simply smiled at her and mouthed, "Wow."

She didn't have time to answer. Someone grabbed her arm and tried to pull her out of the room. She looked up to see Nurse Clarice, who didn't look happy. Did she think Adele caused this? Adele didn't know. But she did know that couldn't leave, not until the man was restrained. She pulled her arm away and stared at him, wondering what he was going to do next. He did nothing. He was still frozen. But now she had to deal with the nurse. She turned and fixed her gaze on her.

"*Quiet,*" Adele said softly. The nurse blinked heavily and swayed a little under the spell. Then she told her, "*Go to your office.*"

"My office?" she said, shaking her head in confusion.

"Now!" Adele said. "Before he wakes up."

"Oh," she said as if she were coming out of a daze.

"Yes, now," Adele said, hoping to send her away so she could put a spell on the room so they would all forget what had just happened.

Nurse Clarice stared at her, then nodded slowly. "I think I have some work to do. Carry on."

"Phew," Adele said. That was one problem taken care of. She waited until she had gone, then threw her hand up and said, "*Be still!*"

Everyone in the room stood motionless. She heard a spoon drop in the kitchen and knew one of the cooks had dropped it after she'd been frozen. Now what? Now what? She looked around at all the girls. She looked at Jane, then at

Lotta and then back to Eliza. Memory erase. She had to erase their memory of this. If she could do that, then no one would know she was a witch and she could get though the rest of the school year and then maybe she could leave for the summer like Jolene had told her.

But then from behind her, she heard clapping. She turned to see Jolene entering the dining room. She grinned at her and said, "Well done."

"What do you mean?" Adele asked. "This is a mess!"

"Messes are for fixing," she said and winked. "And you fixed it."

Adele stared at her and at once realized this was a test. Jolene was testing her!

"You sent him here, didn't you?" Adele asked her, almost wanting to scream her words. But she knew you didn't get anywhere with Jolene through force. You had to sit back and draw her in.

"What if I did?"

"Why did you do it?"

"To show the world what you are," she said and smiled. "Listen, you don't take power like yours and hide it, Adele."

"But you told me to," Adele said.

"Never learned to read between the lines, have you?" Jolene said and sighed. "Well, just to catch you up, the day does come when you can't hide it anymore. And today is your day."

"Jolene, don't do this," Adele said. "Please, don't do this to me right now. I'm not ready."

"But it's time," she said. "It's time to show the world what you are."

"Yeah, but now I'm in big trouble," she said.

"Oh, you are not," she replied, shaking her head. "They're scared of you now. They'll leave you alone."

If that were only true. She shook her head and looked around the room.

"Oh, it's not that hard to do," she said. "Just think about what you need to do and do it. Send him away and then get the girls back in their seats and make them forget."

Adele concentrated on the man and said, "*Go now. Go back to where you belong.*" She watched as he jerked awake and then staggered out of the room and out of the building like he was drunk. She imagined him going to back to a mental institution of some kind.

"Nice," Jolene said then turned to her. "You know, my mother was a witch. Very powerful. She should have known I wouldn't fit in here."

Adele's mouth dropped open. "Why didn't you tell me this before?"

"I don't know," she said. "It just never came up."

Adele shook her head and got back to concentrating on getting the girls to forget. She was about to put the spell on them when she glanced over at Jolene who had a strange look on her face. She asked, "What is it?"

"Nothing," Jolene said then grinned and, before Adele could do anything about it, she shouted, "*Wake up!*"

The girls jerked away and looked around wildly. Then they all stared at her. Adele turned to Jolene. She was almost in tears as she asked, "Why did you do this?"

"You'll find out," she said and gave a wink and disappeared.

It only took the head mistress two minutes to rush in and find out what was going on. When she was told, by Jewel, no less, what Adele had done, she turned her beady eyes on her. Adele wished the floor would swallow her up. It didn't and she knew she was about to be in a world of pain soon.

Head Mistress Tanner didn't immediately confront Adele on her behavior. No, she told everyone to carry on, that there was nothing to be afraid of and to get back to dinner. She ignored Adele as if nothing had happened. But the next day, Adele was summoned to her office. The woman, as usual, was not pleased to see Adele. But today something was different. Today, she did, indeed, have a bit of fear in her eyes.

"Sit down, Adele," she said.

Adele sat.

"Now, tell me what you did yesterday," she said.

"I just told him to stop," Adele said, thinking that was partially true. "That's all."

"That's not all," she said. "You've been doing these things for a while now, haven't you? You've been getting out of work, but the work still gets done. You've been giving the other girls treats, too, haven't you?"

Adele felt panic rise in her but she backed it down. With her newfound power, she knew she no longer had to be afraid of this woman. And she wasn't about to be intimidated, not after what she put her and the other girls through.

"So what of it?" Adele asked.

"What of it?" she snapped. "There are rules and regulations here. This isn't some joke."

"It might not be a joke," Adele said. "But it is wrong what you do to us."

"That's not for you to decide," she said. "And this isn't a discussion we're going to have. I want to know how you did what you did last night."

Adele shrugged. She wasn't about to confess. She was going to stonewall her. The thought of putting a spell on the head mistress occurred to her. She could do that. Maybe a spell that would give her some compassion?

Adele leaned forward a little and stared into her eyes, trying to come up with the perfect combination of spells to really get this woman. As she leaned forward, the locket Jolene had insisted she always wear dangled from her neck. As soon as the head mistress saw it, her face went pale.

"What is that you're wearing?" she asked quietly as if she couldn't quite believe what she was seeing.

Adele ignored her. She was still trying to put the spell on her.

"Tell me what that is!" she screamed, pointing to the locket.

Her voice was so shrill it knocked Adele's concentration off and she was brought back to reality. She stared at her, then at the locket.

"It's just a locket," she said and hoped it was one of those things in her safe that she'd forgotten about. This obviously wasn't going to be the case.

"Give it to me," she said and came around the desk.

Adele leaned back and tried to get away from her but she was determined to get the locket. Adele tried to ward her off with a spell but, because the woman always intimidated her, she couldn't focus. The head mistress made a grab for the locket but Adele finally came back to her magical sense and said, *"Move!"*

The head mistress was thrown across the room. Her back hit the wall and she looked like she'd had the wind knocked out of her. Adele knew she would be in some major trouble because of this.

The head mistress just stared at her. Adele stared back. She didn't know what to do or say right then. This was getting very messy.

"How did you open my safe?" she hissed almost inaudibly. She took a breath and tried again, "Where did you get the combination?"

Adele lied, "In your desk."

"No," she said, getting her breath back. "That combination only exists here." She tapped her head. "I am the only one who knows it."

"Uh," Adele muttered, stalling for time. "Uh... I don't know..."

"Tell me!" she hollered, standing up straight.

Adele blurted, "Jolene!"

The head mistress stared at her for an instant before she screamed. It came out as an animal-like wail and was very unbecoming. Adele was almost embarrassed for her.

"You little liar!" she yelled and crossed over to her and grabbed her arm. "You tell me why you said that!"

"It's true," Adele wailed and tried to wriggle away from her. "Jolene told me."

"There is no Jolene!"

"Yes, there is," Adele said, feeling so bad, so awful.

"Don't let her turn you on me," Jolene said suddenly from across the room. "And don't back down from her."

Adele glanced over at her. She was leaning against the wall, watching the exchange with some satisfaction. She looked like she had been there for a while, too. Adele told her, "But she could hurt me."

"Not you," Jolene said. "You are stronger than she could ever think to be. Use it! Use your magic!"

"I can't think straight!" Adele cried.

The head mistress let go of her arm, then looked around wildly. "Who are you talking to?"

Jolene said quickly, "She can't hurt you. Bind her. Bind her now!"

"I don't want to do that!" Adele cried. "Please don't make me do that."

"Do it or I will," Jolene ordered. "Now!"

Adele turned to see that the head mistress had picked up a small ceramic statue of a milk maid, ready to bash her over the head with it. Adele looked around and noticed the thick, velvet curtains and yelled, "*Bind!*"

The head mistress watched in horror as the curtains bound her, slithering up and around her body like a big, fat snake. Adele breathed a sigh of relief.

"You're the devil!" the head mistress wailed. "Let me out of here!"

Adele just stared at her, not knowing what to do. Jolene walked up and stopped beside her, examining the head mistress.

"The old biddy," she muttered. "Who's helpless now?"

"What am I supposed to do now?" Adele asked Jolene. "Huh?"

Jolene shrugged. "Why don't you ask her how she knows me?"

"Why don't you just appear to her?" Adele asked.

"No," Jolene said. "It's scarier like this. Besides, I can't appear to everyone like I do to you. With her, I'd be more of a mist. More of a ghost."

"What?"

"Just ask her how she knows me, Adele," Jolene said.

Adele stared at her, then at Head Mistress Tanner. "What do you mean? Why do you want me to do this?"

Jolene scoffed. "You think all of our lessons were just for fun? Come on. You had to know that I wanted a payoff."

"And what is your payoff?" Adele asked. "To get me kicked out of here?"

"You'd be so lucky," Jolene said, then stared at Adele. "You're scared to death of her, aren't you?"

"I am," Adele said.

"With all of your power, all the things I've taught you, you're still scared of her? Of *her?*" Jolene was almost beside herself. "I can't believe you!"

"What do you want me to say?!" Adele asked, exasperated. "She's terrorized me!"

"And that's why she's bound right now," Jolene said and sighed.

"And now what?"

"Now we get it out of her," Jolene said.

"Get what?"

"A confession."

"For what?" Adele asked.

"For murdering me," Jolene replied.

Adele didn't even have a chance to respond. Lotta burst into the room just then. Adele turned to stare at her, then Lotta quickly said, *"Disappear!"*

Jolene muttered, "What the—"

But before she could finish, just like that, Jolene disappeared. Adele turned to Lotta, mouth open and held up her hands.

"What was that?" she asked in awe and a little fright.

"I just now realized what was going on," Lotta said. "Tell me, she was here. Right?"

"Who?"

"You know who," Lotta said. "Jolene."

"You know about her?"

Lotta nodded. "I know a lot more than you think I do."

It took some time before things settled down. As soon as Jolene disappeared, three women came into the room. Adele stared at them and knew at once what they were. They were witches, like her. But if she knew that these women were witches, how could she not have known about Lotta?

As if reading her thoughts, Lotta said, "I've been shielded so no one could tell I'm a witch. It's a spell. Unfortunately, it worked in reverse, too because I couldn't figure out what was going on with you and Jolene. She's been teaching you, hasn't she?" She glanced at Head Mistress Tanner and said, *"Undo!"*

The binding spell broke and the head mistress fell to the floor in a slump. She looked terrified but Adele just couldn't find any sympathy for her, mainly because of Jolene's accusation. Could she really have done something to Jolene? Adele wouldn't have put it past her. She had that kind of effect on people; at least she did on her.

"Let's get her settled," one of the women said and all three went and stood over her. They murmured something softly and then the head mistress fell into a deep sleep. They lifted her to the sofa and laid her down. Adele couldn't help but notice that when she was sleeping, she almost looked nice.

"She'll hold for a while until we can figure out what's going on," one of the women said.

"Could someone tell me what's going on?" Adele asked, still feeling overwhelmed.

"Of course," Lotta said and turned to the women. "Adele, this is Nicole, Alexandra and Bea, short for Beatrice."

Adele looked the three women over. They were very sophisticated looking, beautiful and very chic. Alexandra was blonde, tall and thin. Bea and Nicole were shorter and brunette with trim bodies. They were all wearing expensive, mostly black, clothes and very expensive looking jewelry. She would have never been able to tell that these women were witches had she not been one herself. Witches could do that. If Lotta hadn't done that spell to shield herself she would have known she was a witch, too.

"We're sisters," Bea said and pointed at herself and at Nicole.

"Oh," Adele managed to say.

Alexandra, the oldest of the three, came towards her, hand extended, "I'm Jolene's mother."

Adele's mouth dropped and she couldn't utter a word. She managed to shake her hand but she couldn't get her head around what was going on right now.

"Maybe we should explain what's going on," Nicole said and smiled at Adele. "We sent Lotta in to figure it out."

Adele turned to Lotta. "You're not one of us?"

"No," she said.

Adele felt betrayed. While she had never fully trusted Lotta, she did consider her a friend.

"If I could interject," Alexandra said. "Basically, Jolene disappeared years ago and none of us could find her. We were told by the head mistress that she had run away. We, of course, came back here and tried to locate her, her spirit, if you will, so we could find out what happened. However, we could never find her. This has gone on for years and we were at our wits end when Lotta, who's the daughter of a good friend of ours, came to us and said she'd go undercover and see if she could find out what happened."

Lotta nodded. "I've been here almost a year, Adele, and I have never even came close to finding out anything. But soon after you arrived, I started noticing that you were doing weird stuff. Like when you'd go to the restroom during class. You were putting spells on us and the teacher so we wouldn't notice how long you'd been gone. So, I started following you. Sorry, I know that sounds weird, but I had to do it. And I also noticed that you always seemed to be talking to someone who wasn't there and you'd act as though I'd interrupted you. I knew you weren't crazy, but it seemed strange, you know?"

Adele nodded. She wouldn't mention it, but it made sense now that Lotta acted like a hall monitor. She keeping an eye on Adele, trying to find out how she was connecting to Jolene.

"And then, not too long ago, I noticed you were wearing the locket. I have seen photographs of Jolene wearing it. When I saw it, I knew you and she were in contact and I figured she was teaching you magic."

"That sounds about right," Adele said.

"We believe she's using you to do something," Alexandra said.

"Like what?"

"Well, it's her anniversary," she replied.

"Her anniversary?"

"Of her disappearance," she said. "It's been twenty years."

Adele thought about that. She knew that Jolene had died, not just disappeared. How, though, she was still unsure. But what was she supposed to tell these women? She didn't know how she died, not really. Jolene said the head mistress had something to do with it, but how could any of them prove it?

"We think she's dead," Bea said and gave Alexandra a soft look. "But we need closure. We need to know for certain that's what happened."

"It's something the community does," Nicole says. "We have to know what happened to one of ours."

"So, you were told she just ran away?" Adele asked.

"That's what we were told," Alexandra said. "But I'm her mother and I know that she would never do anything like that. Obviously, I've always had a hunch that she's still here, somewhere in this house. I know that now."

Adele nodded.

"I should have never sent her here," she said, her eyes tearing up. "I should have never made her give her baby up."

Adele's mouth dropped. "What?"

Bea cleared her throat and said, "Maybe we shouldn't discuss this."

"No, no, I want to," Alexandra said and turned to Adele. "You see, she was crazy about this young boy, James. And one thing led to another and she got pregnant. I was livid because I, well… I never liked James. There. I said it. I was livid because she was so young and I didn't want her to grow up so fast and I didn't want her to be with him in any way, shape or form. I was a fool. If I had to do it over, believe me, I would have done it better than I did."

"Wow," Adele said.

"So, anyway," she said. "I forced her to break up with him and then he had a boating accident and died. Which was an absolute shock and nearly killed Jolene. But by then the adoption was already set in place and we couldn't back out. I mean, we could have, but not really. But I just thought it was best that she give her baby up."

Adele's head was still spinning. Baby? Adoption? Jolene was someone's mother? Then everything fell into place. Adele suddenly realized that Max wasn't Jolene's brother, he was her son! And he didn't live with Jolene's father, but with his adoptive parents. Why else would she use that kind of power to go see him and to keep in contact with him? It made sense, perfect sense. And she wanted her to know who he was for some reason. That's why she'd taken her to the beach that day.

"You mean Max?" Adele asked her.

"Max?" she asked. "Is that his name?"

Adele nodded. "I thought he was…" She trailed off, allowing other things to fall into place. "I'm sorry, go on."

"Well, after she gave birth and the baby went to live with its new parents, Jolene kind of went wild. She stopped practicing magic and was very out of control. I did some research on Bancroft House and heard they really helped young girls. She begged me not to. She told me she didn't need any help. I never knew she'd never come home from here or I'd never left her."

She burst into tears. Nicole went over and comforted her.

Adele was about to ask a question about Max when, all of a sudden, she felt something. She turned to see the door opening.

"I'm going to get her for that," Jolene said, slamming into the room. She glared at Lotta and started to raise her hand when she saw her mother standing there. She stopped in her tracks and then her whole demeanor changed. Her look softened and her face showed shock and surprise. She murmured, "Mommy?"

"Is she here?" Alexandra asked, her head jerking up. "She's here. I can feel her. Adele, am I right?"

"You're right," Adele said and nodded, not taking her eyes off Jolene.

"Oh, baby, where are you?" she said softly, looking around.

"She's right there, in front of you," Adele said and pointed.

Alexandra squeezed her eyes shut and murmured, *"Reveal, reveal, reveal."*

Jolene's body became very light and then it started to glow. When Alexandra opened her eyes, she could barely see her.

Alexandra cried, "Why didn't you come home to me?"

Jolene looked like she was about to burst into tears, then she turned to Head Mistress Tanner. "Because of her! She kept me here!"

"What is she saying?" she asked Adele.

Adele shrugged, not wanting to tell her. "They can't hear you, Jolene."

"I know," she said. "The time isn't right."

"What does that mean?"

"It just means it's not right," she said and turned to Adele. "You know what you have to do now."

"What?"

"You have to avenge my death," she said.

"I can't do that!" Adele exclaimed.

"You *will* do it," she said. "I gave you all this power for a reason and plan to recoup my investment."

"What is she saying?" Lotta asked.

Jolene turned to her and rolled her eyes and pointed to Lotta. "I knew about her all along. She's not that powerful, Adele. Always remember that."

"Oh, Jolene," her mother said. "We looked everywhere for you. We tried everything. Where did you go?"

Jolene's face hardened and she didn't take her eyes off the head mistress. "Tell her she'll soon find out."

"What that does mean?" Adele asked her.

"It means what it means," she said and disappeared. The soft light was gone.

"Honey," her mother said. "Where are you?"

"She's gone," Adele said.

"She's gone?"

Adele nodded. She was gone and she wouldn't come back until she was ready to take action. Therefore Adele had to take action first. So, she squared her shoulders and turned to Alexandra. "I need you to tell me what happened. I need to know everything."

"Certainly," she said. "Why do you need to know?"

"Because I think Jolene's about to wreak havoc on this school and I have to stop her."

The Story of Jolene

Jolene was sixteen years old when she was brought to Bancroft House and had begged her mother not to leave her there, telling her she got a "creepy" feeling about the place. But her mother was adamant. She said that Jolene needed to be around girls her age, girls who didn't know anything about her or her family or her past. She needed a fresh start and her mother was determined she'd have it.

Right away, Jolene did not like the division she saw amongst the girls. She didn't like the fact that the other girls basically ate slop and leftovers and did all the work while the rich ones lounged their time away. She was very empathetic and tried to be as nice as she could. She was probably the only rich girl who ever said "Please" and "Thank you" to them. It also broke her heart that the other girls were abandoned there by their families. But what upset her more was their treatment by the staff, especially by Head Mistress Tanner, whom she disliked from the moment she laid eyes on her.

However, Jolene decided that it would be best that she kept to herself. Besides, her mother had almost completely bound her power. So, she kept quiet and counted the days until she would be free of Bancroft House. From time to time, she would visit Max, using all the power that she had left in order to do so. When she did this, though, it would completely drain her due to her limited powers. But she didn't care. Whatever it took to go see her son, she would go through. She loved to visit him and watch him play in the ocean. He was still a baby but she could see that one day he would turn into a strong boy and then into a strong man. When he would notice her, he'd come toddling up and fall at her feet. She'd pick him up and hug him, whispering in his ear that one day she'd come back for him and they'd be together. Then she'd return to Bancroft House and pray for the day that she'd be free and able to start her life. Unfortunately for her, her stay there was short lived and she suddenly found herself a ghost.

Being a ghost was hard on Jolene, to say the least. It was like she was stuck in an awful purgatory with girls in pigtails and knee socks. It was also weird because, for the longest time, she couldn't recall how she'd actually died. She remembered the events leading up to her death but it was like time had stopped. The only thing she was sure of was that it was raining that night.

She spent years roaming the halls allowing the young girls to walk right through her as if she wasn't even there. All they would feel is a slight coldness as they passed through her. She didn't yet have the power to fully manifest and that meant she couldn't do anything. She was bored. And this life of being a ghost didn't look like it was ever going to end. The thought of being forever confined to Bancroft House was unbearable.

Ghosts tend to gain their energy from humans. Because young girls have lots of energy and there were lots of young girls at Bancroft House, Jolene soon realized that she was able to take energy from the girls. This meant she could do pretty much what she could when she was alive. It was different, of course, because she was still a ghost. However, she was an intelligent ghost and knew of all the things that were going on. No one knew she was there, of course, and she was able to keep it like that, though she did long for some interaction. She just wanted someone to know she was there, to acknowledge her presence.

It was almost ten years of this when she remembered that she'd brought her *Big Books of Magic for Girls* with her. She remembered she'd hidden it in her suitcase so her mother wouldn't take it from her. She knew the book was there, somewhere in that house. It took her several weeks to locate it but she finally found it in the basement along with all of her things she'd had in her room. She remembered all of the things, like her mary-jane shoes and her plaid wool coat but, as she sorted through her belongings, she felt as if there were something missing. She didn't know what it was exactly but something that had been very precious to her was not there. It took a few minutes of deep thought when she realized that it was her locket. Her locket wasn't in her belongings. Where was it?

She closed her eyes and remembered her father giving her the locket on her twelfth birthday. It was gold and felt solid and good in her hand. It was so special to her, mainly because he'd given it to her just before he and her mother divorced. Now that was something she'd rather forget—all their arguments, all the pain, all the crying.

She shook her head and thought about the locket. Where was it? She couldn't remember. She also realized that because her mother had bound her powers before she died, she might not ever fully get them back. But that's what *The Big Book of Magic for Girls* was for, wasn't it? It took her two weeks of utter and total concentration just to get the book opened. She was a ghost, after all, and most ghosts just didn't have the power to force things to move. But she was different from most ghosts. She had been a very powerful young witch. And this very powerful young witch was tired of being in Bancroft House. She wanted to find a way out.

So, with concentration and effort, Jolene studied the book and got some of her power back. Soon, she found that she could open doors, move objects and frighten the young girls of Bancroft House, which made her giggle with delight. She could take trips outside of the house and, soon enough, she began visiting Max again from time to time. The first time she went to see him, she was afraid he'd be scared of her, or worse, wouldn't be able to see her. She showed up at the motel—that was owned by his adoptive parents—and sat in his room until he came home from school. When he got there, he wasn't even startled. He only smiled and said, "I wondered what happened to you! Where have you been?"

Of course, she had to tell him she was a ghost now. He understood everything without needing to be told every little detail. He was like his father. But she never told him she was his mother though she had a vague feeling that he knew it anyway.

After a few more years of this, Jolene could do a lot of things but she could not permanently leave Bancroft House. No matter what she did, or how far she traveled, she always felt this gravitational pull that pushed her back there. It was beyond understanding. Of all the places in the world, why did she have to stay there? She wanted to be free to roam the world. She wouldn't have even minded staying in Cocoa Beach with Max. But nothing she did could break the chain of the school. She was bound to it in some odd way.

It finally occurred to her one day. She was watching the girls play tennis on the counts in the back of the school. One of them suddenly had a seizure. Jolene watched as the girl jerked and flayed about on the ground. She stared at the white foam coming out of her mouth. She got up, went over and stood next to the girl and the girl recognized her as a ghost. She could see Jolene. And she could see her because she, herself, was coming out of her body and becoming a ghost. She came out and then stood eye to eye with Jolene.

"They can't help me, can they?" she asked.

Jolene looked around at the girls who were flying around trying to help her stay alive. She looked over her shoulder to see Nurse Clarice running across the yard towards the tennis court. And then she looked back at the girl.

"Help is on the way," she told her. "Give it another minute."

"I don't know if I want to," she said and looked up at the sky. "It's so pretty up there."

Jolene stared up and saw, for the first time, the sky opening up, as if to receive this young girl. She couldn't remember that happening for her. *Why hadn't that happened for her?* She turned to the girl and said, "How is that happening?"

"I know how I died," she said and kept her eyes on the sky.

"You had a seizure," Jolene said.

"No," she said. "I got stung by a bee. I'm allergic."

All of a sudden, the girl stopped talking. Jolene stared into her eyes for a moment before they both looked down to see Nurse Clarice stick an epi-pen into her arm. Then she held her until the girl came to. Jolene looked back at her and tried to ask another question but it was too late. The girl was back in her body and she was awake. Soon, an ambulance arrived and she was taken to a hospital and then she came back to school the following day, totally alive and well.

Now Jolene knew why she could never leave this place. She also knew there was a way out and all she had to do was find it. But she didn't know how she'd died. How had she died? What had happened? It stumped her and, when she realized her obvious limitations on finding out, she knew she needed help. And not just anyone would do, either. There was a mystery to solve and a death to sort out.

Jolene began her search shortly thereafter. None of the girls at the school really fit the bill. The girl had to be special and it would help if she was also a witch, or at least was descended from a witch. She knew that this was asking too much, but that's what she needed. Witches didn't just show up at Bancroft House. Regardless, she couldn't be an ordinary girl. This girl had to be extraordinary and, on top of that, she had to have fire in her soul. This girl had to be *exceptional*, even if she didn't have any witch blood.

Girls came and went for a few years. It was so boring. Then Lotta entered the picture. Jolene knew right off that she was a witch and for a few days she was actually excited. It was like an answer to her prayers! But she soon realized that she'd been sent there for some reason connected to Jolene. She wasn't there to free Jolene from her chains of Bancroft House. She was there to séance her, to get her to come out as a ghost. She was, in essence, working for someone else. Her loyalty was not towards Jolene, but for the person who sent her there. Jolene knew that this was an opportunity but she let it pass her by. Lotta wanted answers from Jolene but Jolene knew she couldn't risk it. Lotta was not going to help her. If allowed, Lotta might do something that permanently sealed her fate as a ghost and, if so, there was no way she'd ever be able to leave Bancroft House. On the other hand, a séance might release her, but then what? Then she'd never know what how she died and she needed that closure.

Besides, Lotta bored her.

Jolene was about to give up when she finally saw her. When she saw Adele—even one of her sisters would have been fine—she knew she was perfect. Just the sight of Adele made her smile. *This is the girl! This is the one!* Unfortunately, even with the care of her sisters placed firmly on her shoulders, Adele always had one foot out the door. In fact, Jolene watched as she always looked for any visible exit signs. Of course, there wasn't any. Adele was stuck at Bancroft House and she knew it. Jolene knew that if she ever had the opportunity to leave, she would do so in a heartbeat. This is why she had to make sure she stayed.

And what better way to do that than to instill fear in the girl? She had no fear, not really. Adele was one of those rarities that accepted what happened but didn't let it deter her from what she wanted in life and what she wanted was to be free. Freedom was her currency. She and Jolene were alike in that sense but Jolene had to make sure she never got any.

Since Adele didn't have much fear to begin with, Jolene had to make sure she felt some and one way to do that was to make her a little hungry. Jolene was the one who told the rich girl, Jewel, to trip Adele. It wasn't hard. She just breezed by and whispered in her ear as she passed, *"Trip her. Humiliate her."*

And so the girl had.

It was Jolene that made Jane walk noisily by the head mistresses' room that night, too, rousing her out of sleep. She had to do all of this to keep Adele at her most vulnerable. And when she got her into this position, when she got as low and as hungry as she possibly could, she kicked *The Big Book of Magic for Girls* over to her. Now that was the real test. Was this girl really a witch? Could she be? Did she have ancestors that had, at one time or another, the power? Jolene watched as she dodged the book for a while until finally, she succumbed to it.

And voilà! She had the perfect girl. Not only that, she had a girl who already had some power in her blood. It was the perfect combination. A lonely, poor girl abandoned by her mother who also had witch blood. It was almost too good to be true. All she had to do was guide her, teach her a few things and then, she would be able to manipulate her into doing what she had been waiting years to do—find a way out of this purgatory she'd been sentenced to and figure out what had happened to her.

Of course, it took a while to get Adele to learn to use her power. But Jolene son found that she was actually happy to take the time and actually teach her about being a witch. She taught her how take energy from others if she was ever drained to the point where she needed it. "Just by touch," she said. "And you can replenish your power." Adele asked if it would hurt the other person and Jolene had laughed. "No, you're not draining their blood like a vampire! You're just taking some of their energy. They'll just be lazy for a few hours afterwards."

She taught her everything she knew and, once she got her up to speed, she knew she could utilize her to figure out what had happened. She waited for a sign that would point her in the right direction but none ever came. She began to get frustrated and tired about the whole ordeal and was beginning to wonder if she'd ever know what had happened to her. While Jolene wasn't in a panic to get the mystery uncovered, she knew that her time was running out. She knew that Adele would soon leave Bancroft House and no amount of power or spells would keep her there.

But Adele was not the one who finally unraveled the mystery of her death. Annoyingly enough, it was Lotta. One day, Jolene went into the library to meet Adele. It was late at night and she was about to turn on the lights when she saw Lotta to the side poring over something. Naturally, curiosity overcame her, so she walked over and looked over Lotta's shoulder. Lotta was looking at a big pile of photographs of Jolene. There was one of Jolene at her parents' home. There was one of her riding a rollercoaster. There was one of her and James. Jolene suddenly froze.

Her and James.

Jolene squeezed her eyes shut and forced the memory that began surfacing in her head to go away. Not James. She just couldn't think about him. *James. Oh, dear sweet James.* The memory came to her away. Just after his death, she had tried, without success, to séance him. She had done so many things in order to get in contact with him but nothing worked. In fact, she was starting to dabble more into black magic than she should have. That's why her mother had sent her to Bancroft House. She was afraid of what Jolene might become if she got too entrenched in dark magic.

The thought of never talking to him again was what really got her. She just wanted to talk to him, to tell him she loved him. She paused for a moment and wondered if it were possible for her to talk to him now that they were both dead. But then she realized that he might not be a ghost. He might have made his way into the sky like the girl who got stung by the bee almost did.

She shook her head and concentrated back on the photographs. There was one of her in her school uniform about to mount the steps into Bancroft House. She looked very unhappy. She had begged and pleaded with her mother for days to let her stay home but she was resolved.

A sadness came over Jolene as she stared at the photograph. Lotta had paused on it, too. She might have been seeing the same thing as Jolene was seeing. She might be seeing the anxiety and the depression and the remorse written all over her face. She might be seeing the anger, too, that she had for her mother when she dropped her off. She might be seeing... Wait. What was that?

Jolene leaned over Lotta's shoulder and peered closer. On top of her starched white shirt was something gold. At once, Jolene recognized it. It was her locket. Her hand went instinctively to her chest where it had lain for so many years. As soon as she saw it, everything came back to her. The school. The rich girls. The other girls. The flower factory. Head Mistress Tanner. Head Mistress Tanner. The locket. The locket. Where was the locket?! But then it came to her... Head Mistress Tanner had her locket and the reason she had it hit Jolene like a ton of bricks.

Jolene felt something come over her and could no longer stay in that room. She had to leave. She had to go. But then she heard Adele coming into the room. Lotta's head jerked up and she stared in her direction and, just before Adele came in, made herself disappear. Jolene was actually quite impressed. She hadn't realized Lotta was that powerful.

However, it didn't matter. She had to find that locket and get it. She needed it. The only thing to do was to hang around Head Mistress Tanners' office until she got into her safe. It took about a week before the woman finally opened it. She watched her do the combination and memorized it. Within a matter of days, Adele was wearing the locket.

It was a major coup for Jolene. Now she was on the right track. Now she finally understood how she got to where she was and, more importantly, how she would finally be able to free herself.

Ring Around the Roses

Now, as she stood in front of Cecelia's new house, she knew everything was going to fall into place. Adele was back at Bancroft House trying to figure out what Jolene was going to do. And she knew she was going to try to stop her. That's why she'd come here. She knew Adele would soon be there to play rescuer for her little sister. And that would set into motion the plan that would bring her the freedom she so craved.

"Come out, girls," she called.

Within minutes, the two girls, Cecelia and her new sister, Mabel, came out of the house and joined her on the lawn.

"I know you," Cecelia said.

"You sure do," Jolene said and held out her hands. "Let's play!"

The girls giggled and grabbed her hands and in a circle they went. "Ring around the roses, pocket full of posies, ashes, ashes, we all fall down!"

They fell on the grass and laughed.

"Again!" Jolene exclaimed and they got up and sung it again. The girls didn't tire of the game and around and around they went for what seemed like a very long time. When Adele finally showed up about fifteen minutes later, Jolene was actually relieved to see her. She almost smiled at her. *Look at you now! You've got enough power to travel all by yourself. You're a big girl now, Adele!* But she didn't say anything. She couldn't break her concentration.

"Leave them alone," Adele said.

Jolene smiled and turned to her. "Oh, but we were having so much fun!"

"Leave them alone, Jolene," Adele said, then turned to the girls. *"Freeze!"* The girls stopped moving. She turned back to Jolene. "They've got nothing to do with this."

"Yeah, that's technically true," she said. "But if I don't threaten them, you won't do what I want."

"I won't do it anyway," Adele said. "You can forget it."

"But I can't forget it," Jolene said.

"You will have to."

"If you don't give me what I want," she told her. "I will take what you love."

"You can't do that," Adele said. "You won't."

"Can too. And will. Wait and see."

"No," Adele said and raised her hand. Before Jolene could utter another word, Adele had frozen her.

Jolene looked down at her body, which wasn't moving. She told herself to unfreeze but all she could manage was to get her mouth working. She glared at Adele and said, "Nice try, but I know a lot more tricks than you."

"Whatever you are planning on doing, you will be stopped," Adele said.

"No, I won't," she said and winked. "Watch me!"

Then Jolene literally evaporated. Adele sighed loudly and with annoyance and said, *"Unfreeze!"* to the girls. They woke up and rubbed their eyes. She smiled and crossed over to them, putting her hands on the top of their heads. *"Protect,"* she murmured, then bent down. *"Girls, go into the house and forget what happened."*

The girls eyes glazed over and they obeyed. Adele watched them walk into the house and then breathed a sigh of relief. She was about to go back to Bancroft House when suddenly a big wind began blowing up. She knew what it was and she was about to try and outrun it when it swept her up and carried her high in the air.

"Stop it, Jolene!" she yelled. "Put me down!"

She heard Jolene's laughter and looked down at the ground, which was moving fast beneath her feet. She squeezed her eyes shut and said, "*Down!*" but nothing happened. She couldn't break the spell. She knew there was nothing to do but hold on and just let the wind carry her. Soon enough, she found herself falling into a big, black pit.

When she hit the bottom, she looked up to see Jolene staring at her from above. The hole was more than ten foot deep, not to mention a little scary looking. She yelled, "Let me out of here!"

Jolene shook her head and said, "If you won't help me, I'll do it myself."

And then she disappeared.

Adele screamed, "JOLENE! JOLENE!"

But, of course, Jolene wasn't listening. Adele tried to will herself up and out of the pit but was unable to do so. She realized that she'd used quite a bit of her power saving and protecting Cecelia and Mabel. She would need help and she would need it quickly. She squeezed her eyes shut and started to call out to Eliza but before she did, she realized that Eliza couldn't get her out of the pit. She was small and didn't have the upper body strength she'd need to pull her out. Plus, there would be a lot of explaining to do that she just didn't have the time for. She needed someone cagey, ingenious. She needed someone strong.

"Crap," she said and thought about Jane. Jane was the only person she knew that could help her. But would she help her? Adele had to rely on faith. So, she squeezed her eyes shut and called out her. She imagined her getting the signal and then following her instinct to the pit which she hoped was somewhere on the school grounds.

It took about ten minutes before Adele heard footsteps around the opening of the pit. She hollered, "Jane! Down here!"

A few seconds later, Jane was staring down at her. "Why are you in a hole?"

"Can you help me?" she asked.

"How did you…? How did I…?" She paused and shook her head. "What is going on?"

"I can't explain right now but I have to get out of here," Adele said. "Can you get me out of here?"

Jane stared at her and shrugged. "How on earth can I do that?"

"Figure something out," she said. "And hurry! I don't have much time."

"For what?"

"Just do it! I will explain later!"

"Okay, okay," Jane said and left the pit.

Adele didn't know how much time had passed but soon Jane was back with a rope. She lowered it into the pit and Adele grabbed on and, with Jane assisting her, she climbed out of the hole. It seemed to take forever because she kept falling back as she struggled to get up the steep sides of the pit but soon Adele was out.

Once she was safe, she had to smile at Jane. "Thanks," she said. "I really appreciate it."

Jane nodded. "No problem."

Adele felt remorse at being so cold towards her, mainly because she understood that Jolene had set the whole thing up. She was about to apologize when she heard a commotion. She and Jane stared at each other in confusion, wondering what it was. Then it came to them. It was screams, screams from the girls at Bancroft House.

"Eliza!" Adele yelled and took off running to the school. Jane followed her and soon they found themselves at the back of the school trying to open a door. But it was locked. They ran to another door but it was locked, too, and they soon found all the doors were locked. Adele knew Jolene had secured the school just to keep her out. She stopped and looked around, noticing the darkening sky. Soon, it would be dark and that would mean even more confusion, even more terror.

"What are we going to do?" Jane said, almost in a panic.

"Don't get scared," Adele said. "Let me think. She did this to keep me out. She knows I can beat her."

Jane stared at her. "Who?"

"Jolene," Adele said, not thinking.

"Jolene?" Jane asked. "The girl who got killed here?"

Adele stared at her. "You know about her?"

"Well, to be honest, I just thought it was a rumor or something," she replied. "I never thought it was true. I mean, it is kinda farfetched."

"What happened?"

"Well, it's hearsay, but supposedly, Head Mistress Tanner and Jolene got into a really big fight and she killed her."

"But how is that possible? Didn't the police investigate?"

"Investigate what?" she asked. "I just thought it was a story that somebody made up."

Adele stared at her and suddenly it came to her. She understood what she had to do. "We have to find the body, don't we?"

Jane eyed her. "What do you mean?"

"I mean we have to find Jolene's body."

"Whoa," she said and held up her hands. "I just said that I'd heard of this girl. I didn't mean that I wanted to go look for a body. Besides, the rumor isn't true, right? I mean, Head Mistress Tanner is mean but she's not a killer. Right? Right, Adele?"

Adele realized Jane didn't know anything about what she'd been doing or about Jolene. "It's a long story but, yes, it's true. And Jolene is real. She's a ghost. I've been in contact with her."

Jane stared at her like she she'd lost her mind and was about to say something when they both became conscious of the fact that the screams had died down. It was almost so quiet it was eerie.

They didn't move and listened. There was no longer any sound coming from Bancroft House. That had to mean trouble. If Adele was stronger, she could just burst through the doors but she wasn't. Then she remembered something from the book. She closed her eyes and tried to remember the passage and it came to her, "If, at any time, you feel as though your powers have been drained, know that an enemy is using them against you. In order to regain your power, use your enemy's power against them."

"That's it!" Adele exclaimed then chanted the spell, *"Enemy, enemy, oh, my energy, bring it back, hold it away, sway, sway, sway."* She repeated this three times and then held her arms out and waited until she felt a soft breeze flow to her and then envelop her entire being. Soon enough, all of her power was restored, which meant Jolene's was being drained.

Adele opened her eyes, concentrated on the door and said, "*Open!*"

The door popped open. Jane drew in her breath and said, "Wow!"

"Let's go!"

They entered the school only to find it in complete bedlam. The furniture was all topsy-turvy and paintings were ripped to shreds and the place was an absolute wreck. But there was no sound. Adele looked to her left and saw several girls crouched in a corner looking frightened and confused. *What had Jolene done?* But before she could even begin to answer that question, the girls noticed the open door and made a beeline for it, pushing Jane and Adele out of the way. Adele watched them run and then looked around the hall. It was nearly empty now. She then heard another scream. It was Eliza.

Without thought, she took off running towards her sister's voice and found her at the top of the stairs leaning forward. She was in suspended animation, it seemed, as if she'd been frozen. And she had. She had been attempting to get down the stairs when Jolene froze her and now she couldn't move.

Adele rushed to her, taking the stairs two at a time, and grabbed her, whispering, "*Unfreeze.*" She did and fell in to Adele's arms.

"What is going on?" Eliza asked, breathing heavily.

"I'll tell you later," she told her. "Now I want you to leave. Run as far from this house as you can right now. And I want you to chant this: *'Leave me be, leave me alone, leave me be, leave and be gone.'* Do you understand? Keep chanting that and she can't touch you."

Eliza stared into her eyes and nodded.

"Go now!" Adele said and released her.

Eliza dashed down the stairs and disappeared from sight. Jane stared up at Adele from the bottom of the stairs.

"This is too weird," she said.

"I know," Adele replied.

"Now what?" she asked.

"You need to leave," Adele said. "It's not safe."

"I'm not leaving," she said. "This is the most fun I've had since I've been here."

A scream suddenly erupted from one of the bedrooms. Adele stared towards the sound, then back at Jane.

"We have to find her body," she said. "We have to release her."

Jane shook her head like she was getting overwhelmed. "Like I said, this is too weird."

"You have to concentrate, Jane!" Adele snapped. "We don't have time for this now. We have to find her body."

"But where?" Jane asked. "How can we do that?"

"I don't know," she replied and closed her eyes. Then she knew the only person who would know where her body was had to be Head Mistress Tanner. But first she had to get Jolene under control. She felt her energy flag. She'd used up quite a bit. She opened her eyes and studied Jane. She was probably the strongest girl at Bancroft House. *That's it!* She knew she could take some of her energy and with that energy she could finally get the situation under control.

"I need your energy," Adele said, descending the stairs.

"What does that mean?"

"It means, I need to drain you so I can get this situation under control," she said. "It won't hurt. You'll just feel lethargic. It's what ghosts do; witches can do it, too."

"So, you're a witch?" she asked.

"I am," she said.

"That figures."

Adele resisted the urge to say something sarcastic and said, "Can I have it or not?"

Jane sighed and rolled her eyes then held out her hands. "Take it and put this mean girl ghost to rest."

"She's not mean," Adele said. "She's just pissed off."

"Then she should fit in good around here," Jane said and smiled. "It's no wonder you and her are friends."

Adele rolled her eyes but didn't respond. Then she took Jane's hands, closed her eyes and concentrated. At once she felt Jane's energy course through body. She had a lot, too. The girl was full of good, positive and solid energy. Once she was done, Jane lazily sat propped up against the wall and Adele felt like she could fly. It was one of the best feelings she'd ever had. She smiled before opening her arms and closing her eyes. And then she called to Jolene.

"Come out, come out wherever you are," she chanted. *"Come out, come out, wherever you are... Come out, come out, come out, come out..."*

"That's just so stupid," Jolene said suddenly. "I'm surprised it worked. Your chants really suck, Adele. You need to work on your rhyming."

Adele's eyes popped open. Jolene was sitting on the last step staring at Jane.

"What did you do to Big Red?" she asked and pointed at Jane, who was still sitting against the wall asleep.

"Nothing," Adele said.

"Oh, darn it," she said. "Anyway, I wished I hadn't taught you to do that. This certainly throws a monkey wrench in the plan."

Adele shook her head at Jolene but didn't reply.

"Well," Jolene said, staring at Jane. "At least she's quiet."

Adele sighed loudly. "Why are you doing this, Jolene?"

"You know why, so don't ask stupid questions."

"Why didn't you tell me about Max?" Adele asked.

"How do you know?"

"Your mother broke down and told everyone," she replied. "He's not your brother. He's your son."

"Well, duh," she said.

"You lied to me!" Adele exclaimed.

"I don't have to tell you everything," she said and shrugged.

"Yeah, you kinda do," Adele said. "We're in this together. Or we were."

"Max has nothing to do with you," she said.

"So, your father isn't raising him, is he?"

"No," she said. "My mother was furious about it, about me getting pregnant. She made me give him up for adoption and then she stuck me here." She paused, then continued, "That's why I wanted her here to see the destruction," she said and snapped her fingers.

All of a sudden, the big bouquet of flowers in the foyer burst into flames. Adele silently cursed under breath and put it out. Jolene shrugged and snapped her fingers again. A big

Grecian statue burst into a million pieces. Adele had to duck so the head didn't hit her. She shook her head at Jolene and realized what she was doing. It was time to see what she wanted.

"Tell me what you want," she said.

"I want peace," she said and smiled a little at her. "I've been here so long and it's so boring. You think you had it rough, it's nothing compared to what I've been through."

"Tell me what happened," Adele said.

Jolene's head snapped up and she stared into her eyes. "You wanna know what happened? Then we need to go to the source."

She got up and grabbed Adele's arm. Then they were up off the ground and floating/flying through the air and into the kitchen. There, she sat Adele down and looked around with a pleased smile. Head Mistress Tanner was bound to a chair as were Lotta, Nicole, Alexandra, and Bea.

"Can you believe it? They are some of the most powerful witches on the planet and they were beaten by a ghost! A ghost! That's going to be an embarrassing story to tell."

Adele didn't reply. She stared at them before turning to Jolene, who went to stand in front of Head Mistress Tanner.

"Let's tell them, shall we?" she asked, almost sweetly and then said dramatically, "It was a night long, long ago. Actually, it was twenty years ago today. Remember?"

The head mistress stared at her with wide, wild eyes. She was terrified, as she probably should have been. Jolene shook her head slightly at her and closed her eyes. Then she told the story of what happened.

It had been a long year for Jolene and she just wanted out. She wanted to go home for summer vacation and she wanted to never come back to Bancroft House. She and Head Mistress Tanner had bumped heads on several occasions, particularly over the treatment of the other girls.

But being a student she couldn't really do anything about it. Her mother had bound her powers and she was almost as weak as the other girls. If she'd had her powers, she would have made sure to right the situation. She had fantasies about turning the head mistress into the nicest person on earth. But she didn't know if even she could have done that. The woman was rotten.

However, she had to let it go. She did what she could by being nice to the other girls but for the most part just kept to herself and counted down the days until summer vacation.

On the night it happened, Jolene found that she couldn't sleep, so she got up and went for a walk and found herself outside at the pool, which was in the process of being built. The hole was dug and the tile work was done and it looked like it was going to be a nice addition to the school. She stared at the pool, then sat down on the edge of it, thinking about how nice it would be if there was water in it so she could splash her feet. Then she thought about James and a sharp pain went through her heart. She closed her eyes and wished him well, wished that he hadn't died. She also wished she could have convinced her mother to let her keep Max.

She was so immersed in her thoughts, that she didn't take notice of what was going on at the flower factory. She didn't notice that the lights were still on. She didn't notice anything until she heard the sound of the door being slammed shut.

Her head jerked to the side and she saw Head Mistress Tanner walking away from the conservatory with a man she didn't recognize. They were laughing and talking. Jolene didn't make a sound and listened to what they were saying. They soon made their way towards the house via the pathway that went by the pool.

"No, it's easy, really," the head mistress was saying to the man. "You just promise these poor people that their girls will have the best education and what-have-you, you show them this fancy house and, sure enough, they sign their girls over and their parental rights away."

Jolene couldn't believe what she was hearing.

"It's like we're an orphanage," she continued. "But we get to sell the kids if they're cute enough for someone to want. And, if not, they can work for free in the conservatory. It's a win-win."

"It's a brilliant system," the man said. "However, it will need to be refined."

"Oh, it's getting there," she said. "We've got several new ideas and soon enough they should be up and running."

"It sounds good," he said. "But we need to keep this between us. You understand?"

"I do," she said. "Shall we talk later in the week?"

"I'll give you a call," he said.

As soon as he left, the head mistress turned to make her way into the house but she got a glimpse of Jolene, who was so in shock she couldn't move.

"What are you doing here?" Head Mistress Tanner snapped.

"Nothing," Jolene said nervously.

"Girl, I am warning you," she said. "What are you doing here?"

Jolene stood up and squared her shoulders. She couldn't ignore this. This was wrong! What these people were doing was wrong! How dare they lie to parents just to steal their kids? And then they sell them, too, when they can? It was unbearable, the very thought of it was unbearable. And this woman, Head Mistress Tanner, needed to pay for it.

"Girl," she said. "Tell me what you're doing."

"More like, what are you doing? I mean, I know all about your little flower factory, but this, too? You're lying to people to get young girls in here for free labor! And when you can sell them, you sell them! What kind of place is this?"

"What you don't get, rich girl," she said, almost growling. "Is that this is no concern to you. These girls aren't wanted by their families. They're nothing. No one loves them and they're just in the way. We offer a solution to that."

"And you profit off of it, right?" Jolene asked. "It's wrong. I know that and soon, everyone else will know that, too."

Jolene turned to leave but the head mistress, who'd been thinking ahead, had picked up a wooden mallet which was lying by the pool and hit Jolene's head with it as hard as she could. Jolene probably didn't even feel it, to be honest, as the blow was quick and to the point. Just before Jolene fell back, the head mistress grabbed at her to keep her from falling into the pool but all she got hold of was her locket, which came off her neck. She held onto it as Jolene fell back into the pool and to the bottom. She was out cold. Then it started raining, which roused her. Sheets of heavy rain fell from the sky as Jolene lay in the pool staring up at the twinkling lights from the upstairs bedroom. She couldn't move. She couldn't scream or shout or even talk. She just laid there and let the rain soak her to the bone. The head mistress couldn't physically pull her from the pool to do anything with her body, so she left her there.

Jolene stopped talking as the reality of what she was saying sank in with everyone. No one spoke. The room was silent. Adele stared at her, but knew she wasn't done yet. The worst was yet to come. She wasn't sure what she was going to do, but she had to have patience and let Jolene finish her story.

Jolene glared at Head Mistress Tanner and screamed, "You left me there for hours! I was still alive! You could have saved me! But you left me lying there! In the rain!"

At that moment, massive amounts of rain began to pour from the ceiling, soaking everyone in the room. It was hard to see, hard to know what was going on. This was what Jolene had been after, revenge, and she was going to get it.

"Jolene, stop!" Adele cried.

"No!" she screamed. "Not until that old woman confesses to what she did to me! She knew I was still alive and she let me there to rot! I couldn't move! And do you know what she did? I'll tell you! Before morning, she started burying me! I was too heavy for her to physically move, so she just buried me! While I was still alive!"

Jolene's mother's eyes were wild with fury and disbelief.

"Yes, she started burying me," she continued. "She just started shoveling dirt onto me while I laid there and watched her. I was barely conscious but I remember…" She paused and lowered her voice. "How I died. But that's not the best part. To really make sure that no one ever knew what she did, she had the pool covered in concrete! She told everyone it was a safety hazard. No one questioned it! And no one knew! No one cared! I've been stuck here because I am stuck at the bottom of that hole! I can't leave!"

She can't leave. She can't leave… Stuck in a hole… She can't leave! She's stuck in a hole and she can't leave! That's it! Then it all lined up. That's when Adele knew what to do. Without a second thought, she turned and ran out of the room and through the house and to the back where the pool should have been. She looked around and tried to figure out where a pool would probably be if one existed. Eventually she found the spot. The area was covered by a small, pretty rose garden. Jolene was somewhere beneath there. But she knew she didn't have to actually raise her body to release her. She had to contact her spirit, the part of it that stayed with her body buried beneath the roses. This part of her spirit was trapped and it had to be released.

She sat down in the middle of the garden and started chanting, *"I know you're there, where you lay, come to me and be okay."*

Maybe Jolene was right. Maybe her chants did suck. But they worked and they worked because they got to the heart of the request. That's all that mattered. She continued to chant until she felt something jar the ground beneath her. Adele was about to move when the ground suddenly erupted and she was thrown backwards. She fell on her back and almost passed out from the impact. But she managed to open her eyes and what she saw shocked and mystified her.

It was Jolene, all right. But this Jolene was light and airy and seemed to be all things good. She wasn't human. She was an actual spirit. And she was very happy to see Adele.

"You don't know how long I've waited on you," she said, smiling. "You did it. I knew you'd do it. I knew all along that you would free me."

Jolene stared at her with disbelief.

"Oh, don't be afraid," she said, walking over to her. She smiled and touched her cheek. "I just wanted you to release me, that's all. And now I want to transfer all my power to you. I've been waiting for years, Adele, but now I can be free. And you should have this gift."

"What do you mean?" Adele managed to ask.

"I want to give you my power," she said. "So, come and take it. Take it the way you took Jane's energy. That's all you have to do."

Adele shook her head. She knew what kind of power Jolene possessed and the thought of taking it was terrifying. Too much power might mean lots of problems on down the road and Adele just didn't want that kind of responsibility.

"Please don't make me take it," Adele pleaded. "I don't want it."

"But you have part of it already," she said. "Every single time I've touched you, I've transferred it. You're powerful now, but you will soon be off the charts!"

Adele shook her head. "No, I don't want it. I don't any more power."

"No, it's yours," Jolene said. "I can't take it with me. I have to transfer it onto someone else. It cannot be wasted."

"But why me?"

"Because you're the only one worthy of it."

"No, I can't," Adele said.

"It's a gift," Jolene said. "Take it for the gift it is. Look at it as your reward."

"No! I don't want it!"

"Too late," she said and smiled. "You're already gotten it part of it."

"But I don't know how to contain it," Adele pleaded with her. "I don't want it anymore!"

"It's not a choice," Jolene said and smiled again.

Before Adele could figure out a way to get away from her, she had grabbed her hands and was suddenly transferring all her power onto Adele. Adele stood there and felt this immense energy swell up in her and fill her entire being. It was overwhelming and at one point she thought she'd pass out. Once Jolene had finished, she released her hands.

Adele's body shook and she watched Jolene, who didn't utter another word. Then she simply began to back away from Adele and she kept backing and backing until she disappeared from view. It was like she suddenly just vanished and, maybe, she did. Adele felt a sudden sadness when she realized that Jolene was really gone. She started to run after her, started to call her name, but she knew it would be pointless. She burst into tears. It was like she'd lost her best friend and, really, she had. She hadn't realized how much Jolene meant to her. And not just because they'd shared witchcraft, but because they'd been close. They'd laughed together and she'd cried in front of her and Jolene had consoled her. Jolene had made her life better by just understanding who Adele was. And now Jolene was gone. Adele suddenly felt alone, so alone in the world.

"She's happy now," Alexandra said and laid a hand on Adele's shoulder. "You set her free, Adele. You did what I couldn't. Thank you."

Adele glanced up at her and wiped at her tears. While she was surprised to see the woman standing there, she also felt comfort.

"No, you don't have to stop crying," Alexandra said and smiled at her, smiled though her own tears.

"I'm just going to miss her so much now," Adele said. "Weird, huh? She used to kinda get on my nerves."

She nodded. "My daughter was very persuasive," she said. "If I had only known…"

She trained off and looked in the direction that Jolene had disappeared. Adele stared too, then Alexandra sat down besides her.

"Adele," Alexandra said. "Your life is about to change."

Adele nodded. She knew that she was now a very powerful witch. She felt it in her bones. She felt different. She knew her life would be different now. She glanced over her shoulder at Bancroft House. Yeah, it was over but something new had only just begun.

A New Life

The authorities were contacted and the staff was taken away and Bancroft House was closed. The rich girls were sent home and the other girls were sent to foster families and into state care and some to live with relatives. Some were even adopted.

It was a big scandal. How could something like this happen in this day and age? Well, the answers were easy. Places like Bancroft House happen because tragedy strikes unsuspecting families and puts them in desperate mindsets. When this happens, there's always someone ready to take advantage. That's all.

Alexandra promised to keep in touch and said that she would always be there if Adele needed her in the future. She also told her that she would need help, real help, to keep her powers in check. That's why it was an obvious choice that Nicole and Bea, who were good friends with Alexandra, adopt Adele and Eliza. Adele was very happy at the prospect but told them they didn't have to do it out of sympathy or obligation. To which they responded that they, certainly, would have never done that and they wanted to help the girls not only out of genuine concern but because neither of them had kids of their own. They also wanted to keep a watch on Adele's newfound powers and loved the thought of having Eliza live with them, as well. They were nice women and they sincerely cared about the Clemmons girls.

Of course, Adele hated the thought of leaving Cecelia. But Nicole and Bea assured her that once she and Eliza were settled in their new home, they would speak to their family lawyer and see what could be done about the situation. It was a process that might take some time, but they were confident that something could be done to enable them to stay in contact with their sister. But to take her out of her home was out of the question. Cecelia was in love with her new family and to tear her away from them would have repercussions. It was best to tread lightly at first and then proceed with bi-monthly visits, at the very least.

Adele and Eliza's new home was an old Gothic revival style house that looked like an old church, one that a person might find in a storybook. It had the pitched roof and gables and a big double front door painted black to match the roof. It was so cool, Adele gasped when she first laid eyes on it.

"Is it a church?" Eliza asked.

"No," Bea said, laughing. "It's not."

The house was so grand—and so cool—it looked unreal. It was a few hundred miles west of Bancroft House, near Nashville, and sat on over a hundred acres. Inside, the floors were old, well-worn and beautiful oak. The walls and ceilings were plaster with ornate moldings. The chandeliers were so fancy and sparkly they seemed to wink at Adele and Eliza. It was just the coolest house they'd ever seen and they were so happy that it was going to be their home. The girls just couldn't get over their luck.

Eliza and Adele stood looking around the immense living room, mystified that they were going to be living in such a house. Then Eliza turned her gaze on Bea and Nicole and asked, "Why aren't you married?"

"We're old maids," Bea said, laughing.

"We're not *that* old," Nicole snapped. "But seriously, Adele, you have to realize that being a witch does come with a price. Men just don't get it."

"Get what?" Eliza asked.

"Get the fact that your work will always take precedence over them," Bea said.

"I'm glad I'm not a witch," Eliza said.

"Not yet, anyway," Nicole said and winked at her.

Eliza turned to Adele with a mortified look on her face. Everyone burst out laughing.

"They're just joking with you, Eliza," Adele said, wiping at her eyes. "Calm down. No one is going to make you do anything."

"Let's go into the kitchen and have something to drink and then you girls can get settled in your rooms," Nicole said.

They followed her into the large kitchen which was as breathtaking as the rest of the house.

"Your house is magnificent," Adele told Nicole.

"Thank you. We inherited it from our parents," Nicole said.

"And they inherited it from their parents," Bea added, opening the refrigerator door. She took out and big pitcher of lemonade and poured everyone a glass. After they were served, she held hers up and said, "Here's to a new life!"

"A new life!" Adele said and took a sip. Umm… Good lemonade.

"I think you girls are going to like it here," Bea said, smiling at them.

"I think you're right," Adele replied.

"Now your rooms are just upstairs and to the left," Nicole said. "They're our old rooms, so if you don't like the color schemes, we can redo them."

"I'm sure they'll be fine," Eliza said.

"Good," Bea said and pointed at Adele's glass. "Take it with you to your rooms. You girls need to get unpacked. Supper is six."

"Thanks," Adele said. "Come on, Eliza."

She and Eliza sipped the delicious lemonade on the way to their rooms, which were side by side. Eliza grinned and went into hers and then Adele went into hers, closing the door softly behind her. When Adele looked around her room, she smiled with pride because she realized that this was the first time she'd ever had her own room. And what a magnificent room it was. It was long and wide with tall ceilings that were flanked with not one but two fans for those hot summer nights. It had a huge antique four-poster bed in the middle with two mahogany nightstands. There was a sitting area in front of the big picture window and a soft, warm rug beneath her feet. In addition to the room being so wonderful, it had its own en-suite bathroom, which made it that much better.

She was about to lie down on the bed and smile at her good fortune when she heard a noise. She turned. Jolene sat on her bed, swinging her legs. She was reading a book. This one was called *A Season in Hell*.

"Rimbaud," Jolene said and tossed the book to the side. "I don't suppose you know anything about him, either."

Adele's mouth dropped.

Jolene ginned and said, "You're surprised to see me. I get that. But you didn't really think you were going to get rid of me that easily, did you, Adele?"

Adele dropped the glass of lemonade but managed to say, "Oh, brother, you've got to be kidding me."

Printed in the USA
CPSIA information can be obtained
at www.ICGtesting.com
LVHW090758180124
769297LV00007B/116